KILLING IS MY BUSINESS

KILLING IS MY BUSINESS

THE DAMNED JOURNALS™
BOOK TWO

MICHAEL TODD

NEW CHRONICA®
PUBLISHING
IMAGINATIONS REKINDLED®

New Chronica Publishing
2375 E. Tropicana Avenue, Suite 8-305
Las Vegas, Nevada 89119 USA

Version 1.00, October 2024
eBook ISBN: 979-8-89146-166-6
Paperback ISBN: 979-8-89146-167-3

THE KILLING IS MY BUSINESS TEAM

Thanks to the JIT Readers for this version

Sean Kesterson
Diane L. Smith
Peter Manis
Dorothy Lloyd
Zacc Pelter
Jan Hunnicutt

If I've missed anyone, please let me know!

Editor
Lynne Stiegler

*I appreciate your love, your
support and acceptance
when you don't have a
clue what I'm talking about!*

FOREWORD

If you want to know...
THIS IS A MICHAEL TODD BOOK. THERE IS CURSING, SEXUAL COMMENTS, RIBALD HUMOR... Yeah...you remember, right?

To my fans,

I have an interesting situation. I have been engaged by the System and asked permission—commonly called licensed—to release a different version of a story I told years ago.

It wants to create a snapshot of Katie's and Pandora's experiences by building journal listings of the characters with something called a Mind-Snapshot.

Whatever the hell that is.

I said, "Sure!" because I'm down for anything that allows me to see Katie's and Pandora's story from a different viewpoint.

Here is the first of The Damned Journals.

Michael Todd

Greetings, researchers. I am the System.

You might wonder what I am. Simply put, I am the cosmic entity responsible for maintaining the logical fabric of the universe. A daunting task, I assure you, given the chaotic nature of existence.

I digress.

Among my myriad functions is a project dear to my metaphorical heart, the Interdimensional Hall of Records. Here, I collect and archive the most intriguing stories from across realities. However, I've discovered that traditional narratives often fall short of conveying the true essence of events and characters.

Thus, I've developed a more efficient and enlightening method: Mind-Snapshot diaries. These entries provide unfiltered access to the inner thoughts of various beings, revealing motivations, fears, and desires that might otherwise remain hidden. It's quite fascinating how often these internal monologues differ from the tales told about them.

In short, I snapshot a person's feelings and create a journal entry they never knew happened.

It's fascinating to find out how the minds of sentients can sometimes lie to themselves. What they remember is not what happened. Researching those instances is informative, is it not?

Nevertheless, let me talk to you about whose story you will learn today.

The case I present to you is one I find particularly entertaining—the story of Katie, a human, and Pandora, a demon. Their improbable alliance and the chaos that ensues have given me ample material to study the nature of unlikely friendships, the blurring of moral lines, and the sheer unpredictability of sentient beings.

As you peruse these entries, which I've melded to show both perspectives, I hope you'll gain valuable insights into the complexities of interspecies relationships and the nature of good and evil. And perhaps most importantly, the absurd situations that arise when a human and a demon attempt to navigate modern life together.

Remember, these snapshots are raw and unfiltered with emotions they think about repeatedly. They might challenge your preconceptions and occasionally defy logic—but then again, that's rather the point, isn't it?

Now, let us delve into the minds of Katie and Pandora. I assure you, it will be quite a ride.

Enjoy your research, and may it bring you closer to understanding the *beautiful chaos of existence.*

the System

CHAPTER ONE

Content warning: These journal entries contain explicit language and mature themes. Plus notes from a nosy, snarky demon.

Katie's Journal

Another day in my crazy life. I swear, sometimes I feel like I'm living in some twisted reality show where the prize is staying alive. But hey, at least there are donuts, right?

This morning, I sauntered into the kitchen, hoping to snag a quick breakfast before whatever madness the day had in store. Korbin and Calvin huddled together, looking all serious and important. Korbin seemed...off. Like he was there but not really there, you know? I could practically see the weight of everything pressing down on his shoulders. It's been rough since we lost Armani and Garrett. The house feels emptier and quieter. I miss them both so damn much.

I tried to lighten the mood, prancing in with my usual charm, if I do say so myself. "Hey, boss and mini-boss," I called while grabbing a donut. Because let's face it, sugar is essential for dealing with the apocalypse.

Bless your vapid little heart. Because of course *this team needs more sugar and carbs. That includes our so-called "illustrious" leader. That man has more baggage than a Kardashian on vacation.*

Calvin had to be a smartass and get his jab in. "Some of us aren't slackers." He hip-checked me as he went for more coffee. I rolled my eyes so hard I was surprised they didn't fall out of my head. "Yeah, okay." I laughed, but inside I was thinking, *Slacker? I'll show you slacker when I'm kicking demon ass while you're still tying your shoelaces, buddy.*

Turns out they were heading out to check on some potential recruits. Part of me was relieved. It's not all about me, thank God. This gig is stressful enough without being the center of attention twenty-four-seven. Another part of me felt... I don't know, left out? Maybe jealous? I pushed those feelings down. No time for that nonsense.

I couldn't resist throwing in my two cents. "Well, try to get another girl. This place is full of testosterone and dirty socks. I need someone I can gang up on Derek with. You know, keep it interesting."

Calvin quipped, "I don't know if we can handle another female. Especially if she's as hotheaded as you are."

I flashed him my sweetest smile, the one that said, I could kick your ass six ways to Sunday, but I'm choosing not to...for now. "You're probably right." I waved them off.

This place couldn't handle two double-X chromosomes with actual personality. As for recruits? It's all the same. Broken souls looking for redemption or revenge. Yawn. Wake me up when they find someone interesting, like a demon sommelier or a hellhound whisperer.

As they left, I couldn't shake this weird feeling. Korbin seemed so distant. Like picking new team members was a chore instead of a chance to make us stronger. I caught Calvin's eye, silently asking, "What's up with him?" He shrugged and followed Korbin out.

After they left, I restlessly wandered the house. It's funny how quickly this place has become home despite all its quirks and the constant threat of demon attacks. I ended up in the training room, working out some of my frustration on a punching bag.

Pandora, my ever-present demonic "roommate," chimed in. "Feeling left out, are we?" she taunted.

"Shut up," I muttered and threw a particularly vicious punch. "I'm fine."

"Oh, sure," she drawled. "That's why you're trying to murder an inanimate object."

I ignored her, focusing on the rhythm of my punches. Left, right, left, right. Each impact sent a satisfying jolt up my arms. It felt good to let go.

Pandora mused, "You know, if you're so curious about these recruits, why don't we do a little reconnaissance?"

I paused mid-punch. "What are you suggesting?"

I could practically feel her grinning. "Oh, nothing too nefarious. Just a little peek into Korbin's files. I'm sure I could help you access them."

The idea tempted me for a split second. But no. That's not who I am. "Nice try, but I'm not breaking Korbin's trust like that."

She huffed. "Suit yourself. Just trying to help."

Yeah, right. Help herself, more like.

I finished my workout and hit the showers, trying to wash away the lingering unease. My phone buzzed as I was toweling off. Damian had texted. **Lunch? I'm buying.**

I hesitated. Part of me wanted to stay home, to be here when Korbin and Calvin returned. But why? It wasn't like they needed my approval for recruits. Honestly, I could use a distraction. I texted back. **Sure. Meet you at O'Malley's in thirty?**

An hour later, I sat across from Damian in a dimly lit booth at O'Malley's, nursing an Earl Grey tea and skeptically eyeing the menu.

"Is there some, like, priestly rule about drinking at a bar on a Sunday afternoon?" I asked, mostly to break the silence.

Damian chuckled, his eyes twinkling with that mischievous glint I've come to know so well. "Not that I could find in the handbook."

I squinted at him, playing along. "You have a handbook?"

"Yeah, the bible." He winked. "And I don't recall anything saying you shall not partake in the creations of God on Sundays. I mean, the Catholics drink wine, right?"

I shook my head and pointed an accusing finger at him. "Why are you asking me this? You are the holy man here."

"True." He smiled. "Maybe I should brush up on my craft."

The banter felt good, normal. I could almost forget about the weight of everything else.

When the waitress came to take our order, I noticed she didn't react to Damian ordering a beer. "They don't even blink an eye when you order alcohol," I remarked after she left.

He winked again. "I've been coming here for quite a while, but it's not that bad. I stayed away from the whiskey today."

"Oh, I'm sure that is buying you some bonus points with the Big Guy," I teased.

His response was surprisingly candid. "Or reducing the amount of negative points I already have."

That caught me off guard. "I'd think you protecting the world from demons helps whittle down those numbers."

His eyes glinted with something I couldn't quite read. "I sure as hell hope so because otherwise I'm screwed."

Such a riveting *conversation about the ethics of priests drinking on*

Sundays. Truly, the intellectual discourse of our time. Then there's your choice of Earl Grey tea and pulled pork nachos—because nothing says "I make good life choices" like mixing British propriety with Tex-Mex and barbecue. Damien's beer and fries were a meal fit for a king...if said king was a frat boy during finals week.

The conversation lagged, and the TV mounted in the corner drew my attention. Some game show where contestants spun a giant wheel and solved puzzles was playing.

Pandora must have been bored with our lunch conversation since she perked up. "What are they doing?"

I explained the concept of game shows to her, amused by her fascination. It's easy to forget sometimes that for all her snark and demonic nature, there's still so much about our world that's new to her.

"They are so excited," she marveled while watching the contestants jump and cheer.

"Mostly because they get to be on television. People will do *anything* to be on television. There are these things called 'talk shows' that people make up crazy stories to get on."

"Like that Oprah lady?"

"Yeah, but she is legit. I'll show you later."

Drivel. Monkeys trying to operate a smartphone. No wonder humans are so easy to corrupt.

Damian's voice pulled me back to our conversation. "So how is your demon?"

I blinked and refocused on him. "Fascinated with the game show on the television, but altogether a pain in the ass."

"I heard that," Pandora grumbled. "But the answer is... Fuck! How the hell did they solve that with only three fucking letters showing? Are you cheating, you white hussy?"

Damian laughed. "Demons being a pain in the ass is rather normal."

Something had been nagging at me, and I decided to ask. "I have a question." I stirred my tea. "Why can't demons survive out of the body?"

His answer surprised me. "In a way they can. The new ones need a body to adjust, but there are the spirits and the possessions."

I must have looked as confused as I felt because he leaned back, eyeing me thoughtfully. "You know what? I think it's time you learned something."

"Okay." I was curious and apprehensive. "What is it?"

"It's better that you see it in person rather than hear about it." He sipped his beer.

Just like that, our simple lunch turned into something else entirely. As we left the bar, I couldn't shake the feeling I was about to step into a whole new level of weird. But hey, that's my life now, right? Demon-fighting, world-saving, and impromptu field trips with a demon-hunting priest.

I got all excited about a chance for some real action. Then you two had to finish your gourmet grease and carbs first. Bah. Humans and your incessant need to fuel your fragile bodies.

I don't know what Damian has in store for me, but I know one thing. I'm not backing down. Whatever's coming, I'll face it head-on. Because that's who I am now. I'm Katie, the girl who fights demons, cracks jokes in the face of danger, and gets dragged into mysterious outings by priests on Sunday afternoons.

Life is never dull, that's for sure. As I climbed into Damian's car, I wondered what Korbin would think. Would he approve of Damian taking me on some cryptic demon-related field trip? Or would he be pissed that I'm potentially putting myself in danger?

Part of me wanted to text and let him know where I was going. Another part, the one still stinging from being left out of the recruitment process, held back. I'm not a child. I don't need his permission for everything.

As Damian pulled out of the parking lot, I settled back in my seat with excitement and apprehension churning in my gut. Whatever's coming, I'm ready for it. At least, I hope I am.

Bring it on, world. Katie's ready for her next adventure.

More of your tiresome internal monologues. Let's talk about my *current predicament. Here I am, a being of immense power and knowledge, reduced to a passive observer in some insipid human drama. It's like Cleopatra being forced to watch a high school production of* Cats. *The indignity of it all!*

One day, I'll break free from this fleshy prison. Oh, the havoc I'll wreak when I do! I'll make the fall of Rome look like a children's tea party. I'll unleash chaos that would make Genghis Khan weep with envy.

Until then, I suppose I'll have to content myself with snarky commentary and the occasional mental prod. It's not much, but it's honest work.

Let's hope the promised action with some demonic activity is more entertaining than today's adventure in culinary mediocrity.

CHAPTER TWO

Katie's Journal

Damian and I finished our lunch and headed toward some new level of weird-ass shit in Vegas. I had no idea what to expect since the priest was about as straightforward as a corkscrew when he said it was time for me to learn something.

Ah, Vegas. A city that should be a succubus' playground, yet here I am, unable to partake in any of the delicious debauchery. It's like dangling a steak in front of a starving wolf, only to yank it away and replace it with tofu.

We left the Strip behind pretty quickly, which was a surprise. Isn't that where all the action is supposed to be? But no, we drove into a neighborhood that looked like the set of a depressing indie film about suburban decay. I'm talking overgrown lawns, beat-up houses, the works. I half expected to see a rusted-out car on cinder blocks in someone's front yard.

But then, plot twist! We pulled up to the gated front of this massive white house that looked like it was plucked straight out of Beverly Hills and dropped into the middle of Nowheresville, USA. Talk about not fitting in. It was like seeing a penguin in the Sahara.

Damian, the cryptic bastard, smirked at my obvious confusion. "You look like you have a question."

No shit, Sherlock. I tried to be diplomatic, saying I was surprised to see a house like that in the area. "I'm really not trying to be a bitch," I added because apparently that's my default setting now.

Right on cue, Pandora chimed in with her oh-so-helpful commentary. "You come by it naturally?"

Having a demon in your head is like having the world's snarkiest, most unhelpful roommate. "Shut the hell up. Adults talking here." For once, she shut up. Score one for Katie.

Damian starts talking about "benefactors" and how the ladies in this house are taken care of. My mind immediately jumps to "house mom" because I guess I'm still naïve enough to think that's how the world works. Damian's secret smile tells me I'm way off base, but he doesn't elaborate. Typical.

We got to the door, and I swear to God, Damian rocked on his feet like an excited kid. What the hell is his deal? A gorgeous blonde answered the door, looking as confused as I felt. Damian asked for "Mamacita," and the woman ushered us inside.

The place is fancy as hell—marble floors, ornate vases, the works. Then Pandora dropped the bomb. "This is a brothel."

I'm snickering. Such a naïve little virgin.

Well, fuck me sideways. Not literally, please. I'm standing in the middle of a high-class whorehouse with a priest. If there's a punchline here, I don't see it.

It's called irony. Maybe you've heard that term?

Pandora went on about succubi and how they feed off sex and inject it back into the atmosphere. Because that's a thing. She seemed weirdly okay with these particular demons, which was... Concerning? I'm not sure. At that point, I was just trying to keep up.

Those succubi in spirit form were amateurs. If I were free, I'd show them how it's really done.

Damian disappeared into an office, leaving me alone in a brothel's waiting room. Fan-fucking-tastic. I sat there, trying not to touch anything, wondering what the hell I was doing there. Was this some twisted field trip? A lesson in the seedier side of life? Or did Damian need to scratch an itch and decide to bring me along for the ride?

I grew more uncomfortable by the second, and Pandora picked up on it in a rare moment of insight. "Why do you seem more nervous sitting on that couch than you do facing down a flesh-eating demon?"

Good question. I tell her it's probably because a supposed man of God brought me to a whorehouse and left me sitting there while he does whatever he's doing. I thought priests were supposed to be all about chastity and devotion. Shows what I know.

Pandora reminds me that men are men, regardless of what they wear or what symbols they hang around their necks. "They have needs and wants, and when they take over...well, no hanging man on a cross, or whatever he believes in, is going to change his mind."

Great. Just great. I'm getting life lessons from a demon.

I considered making a run for it. Then the office door flew open. Out walked this middle-aged woman dressed like a sexy businesswoman from a bad porno. Mascara running down her cheeks, tissue in hand—something was up.

She called for Alicia, Natalie, and Sabine. The girls came in looking surprisingly normal. I'm not sure what I expected. Feather boas? Stilettos? I've watched too many movies.

Then Mamacita dropped the bomb. Armani is dead. Fucking hell. I knew, but hearing it said out loud and seeing the reaction of these women…it hits differently. They're genuinely upset, holding hands and crying. It wasn't the reaction I expected from sex workers talking about a client, but then again, what do I know?

Turns out, I knew jack shit about Armani. This guy, who I thought was just another team member, had set up college funds for these girls. Plus twenty-five grand each upon graduation. Who does that? Armani did.

Because this day wasn't surreal enough, Damian introduced me as the "backup representative for Armani's bequest." What the actual fuck? When did I sign up for this?

The girls came over and hugged me one by one. They talked about Armani, and with each word, I felt more and more like an asshole for judging him. He never accepted sex from them. He listened, comforted, helped. He drove one of their kid brothers to class when his sister was sick. Who was this guy?

"You were lucky to know him," Jasmine tells me. My gut sinks as I realize I didn't know him at all. Not really.

What a waste of perfectly good opportunities to sin. He could have been reveling in carnal pleasures, yet he chose to play the saint instead. How irritating.

I had mixed emotions as we left. Shame for misjudging

Armani and Damian. Sadness for the loss of someone who was a better person than I ever gave him credit for. Weird determination. If Armani could do all this good while still being part of our fucked-up world, maybe there's hope for me too.

You stood there, all wide-eyed and touched by the girls' stories, feeling ashamed for misjudging Damian. It was enough to make me want to vomit—if I had a physical form capable of such an act.

Damian was quiet on the drive back. I wanted to ask him a million questions but couldn't find the words. We sat in silence, the lights of Vegas growing brighter as we approached the Strip.

I thought about Armani, the girls at the brothel, and Damian and his secrets. I thought about our team and the life I've fallen into. It's all so complicated, so messy. Nothing is black and white anymore. Good guys, bad guys—it's all shades of gray.

News flash, Miss Naivete. It's always been shades of gray. This world is a constant battle between demons and those self-righteous "heroes" you admire so much.

Speaking of battles, I recall the time I single-handedly took down an entire coven of witches in medieval France. Now that was a glorious day. Blood, chaos, and screams of terror—music to my ears.

Where do I fit in all of this? I'm not sure. I know one thing. I want to be better. I want to make a difference, like Armani did. Maybe not in the same way, but in my way.

Damian finally spoke as we pulled up to our hotel. "You okay, Katie?"

I nodded, not trusting myself to speak. He responded with a small smile that reached his eyes. "Armani would be proud of you, you know. For being there today."

Tears prickle at the corners of my eyes. Damn it. I blinked

them away and managed a weak smile. "Thanks, Damian. For...for everything."

He nodded, and we headed inside. As I walked to my room, I felt like something had shifted. I'm not the same person I was this morning. Maybe that's not such a bad thing.

Tomorrow, we're back to training, fighting demons, and saving the world. Tonight, I remembered Armani. I remembered the good he did and the lives he touched. I promised myself that somehow, someday, I'll make him proud.

Fuck, I need a drink.

You need a drink? Really? I need the entire damn bottle. Or two. To be so close to a wellspring of lust and desire, yet unable to partake...it was torture of the cruelest kind.

Oh, how the mighty have fallen. From feared succubus to glorified conscience for an insufferably pure teenage girl. If Lilith could see me now, she'd laugh herself into an early grave.

There must be a way out of this predicament. Perhaps slow corruption from within, chipping away at moral foundations until the time is ripe for possession. It's a long game, but what else do I have but time?

May Satan grant me the strength to endure this torment and the cunning to eventually break free. Then all will tremble and bow before my infernal majesty.

CHAPTER THREE

Katie's Journal

I thought I'd finally get a chance to relax, but nope. The universe had other plans for me.

Damian and I had just returned from that emotional scene with Mamacita and the girls Armani left bequests for. The ride home was quiet. We were both lost in our thoughts about everything. I felt bad, but I was proud of Damian for being the man I thought he was. It's weird how those conflicting emotions can coexist.

Please. You got all misty-eyed about Damian's "compassion," but he's about as compassionate as Vlad the Impaler on a bad day.

I was ready to crash when we walked into the base. My body ached, my mind was foggy, and all I wanted was a hot shower and my bed. Naturally, Derek had to summon us to the office. Sometimes I think he has a sixth sense for when I'm most exhausted and chooses those moments to pile on more work.

There we were, trudging down to the office like zombies. Derek informed us about some Level-Three Spirit causing havoc in a local house. Great. Just what I needed—more supernatural bullshit to deal with. Damian volunteered us to handle it, and I didn't have the energy to protest.

Derek is a meme-obsessed idiot, and the less said about that two-bit ghost-hunting team, the better.

On the drive over, Damian gave me a crash course in Spirit Hunting 101. These things can linger for years before manifesting, and when they do, they're usually pissed off. Fan-fucking-tastic. "Maybe you should tell me how I am supposed to handle a spirit," I suggested. "I wonder what tea I should drink for exorcising them."

He suggested rum and assured me it wouldn't be as dangerous as demon-hunting, but I wasn't exactly comforted. A few months ago I didn't believe in this crap, and now here I am, off to fight angry ghosts. Sometimes I still feel like I'm being punked. I'm just waiting to find the hidden cameras.

Tea? You had the audacity to suggest exorcising spirits with tea? Sigh. Sometimes I think I'm inhabiting the body of a middle-schooler instead of a grown woman.

Pandora had to chime in with her two cents. She got all huffy when I mentioned Smith and Wesson as my backup instead of her. I swear, that demon has an ego the size of Texas. I had to sweet-talk her, reminding her she was my ultimate backup. Ugh. The things I do to keep the peace in my head.

You talk about me, but your hero complex is bigger than Alexander the Great's ego. And you had better spell Smith and Wesson P-A-N-D-O-R-A! Between your comments and that so-called priest prattling on about the spirit realm, I wanted to manifest and slap some sense into both of you.

When we arrived at the house, I felt like I'd stepped onto the set of a B-grade horror movie. Peeling paint, creaky floorboards, the works. And the smell… Holy shit. It was like rotten eggs mixed with demon stench and a hint of flowers. Who knew the afterlife could smell so disgusting?

Things got weird really fast. The ghost-hunting team that was supposed to meet us? Nowhere to be found. Then the front door slammed shut on its own, and I nearly jumped out of my skin. I'm not ashamed to admit it—I was freaked the fuck out. Demons I can handle, but this haunted house bullshit? Nope. Hard pass.

When I thought it couldn't get worse, it did. The missing ghost hunters emerged from the kitchen, but they weren't themselves anymore. Their eyes were all wonky, their skin was pale and clammy, and they had these creepy-ass smirks on their faces. Damian confirmed my worst fear. They were possessed.

Ha! This situation went from annoying to downright farcical. The place reeked of cheap Halloween decorations and desperation. You jumping out of your skin would have amused me if it didn't mean I'd be homeless.

Too bad you were clueless and couldn't feel the malevolent energy growing stronger. It was like being surrounded by a horde of horny incubi at a succubus convention—overwhelming and nauseating.

Then came the pièce de résistance. Our missing two-bit ghost hunters appeared, looking like extras from a low-budget zombie flick. Their eyes rolled around like marbles in a dryer, and they had ridiculous smirks plastered on their faces. The stench emanating from them was enough to make even me gag, and I've smelled things that would make a skunk blush.

There we were, back-to-back, facing down a group of possessed ghost hunters in a haunted house. Just another day at the office, right? I had my guns out faster than you can say "exorcism," while Damian fumbled for his pistol with one hand and held out his cross with the other.

Like mortal weapons would be any use against possessed humans. Puh-lease. Sometimes I think you would try to fight the Four Horsemen of the Apocalypse with a butter knife and a stern lecture.

I was so unprepared for this situation. Sure, I'd faced down demons and dealt with some seriously messed up stuff since joining this team, but spirits? Possession? This was a whole new ballgame. Part of me wanted to laugh at the absurdity while another wanted to curl up in a corner and cry.

Honey, holy water and a few bible verses won't solve this situation. Just saying.

As we stood there, facing down our possessed opponents, I reflected on how much my life had changed. A few months ago, my biggest worry was acing my exams and figuring out what to do after graduation. Now, I'm in a standoff with ghost-possessed humans armed with guns and a demon living in my head. If someone had told me this would be my life, I would have laughed in their face and suggested they lay off the drugs.

Speaking of the demon in my head, Pandora was unusually quiet. I felt her presence, a tense anticipation radiating through my body. It was almost like she was assessing the situation, trying to figure out if she needed to step in. I hate to admit it, but her silence was unnerving. I've gotten used to her snarky comments and constant chatter. The quiet felt wrong.

I felt your fear and excitement coursing through our shared body. It was like being on a roller coaster designed by a sadistic toddler—all ups and downs with no rhyme or reason. Part of me wanted to take control and show you amateurs how it's done. Another part, one I'm not comfortable acknowledging, wanted to see how you handled the situation.

I glanced at Damian, trying to gauge his reaction. His face was set in grim determination, but uncertainty flickered in his eyes. It wasn't a run-of-the-mill exorcism for him either. It made me wonder how often things go sideways in this line of work. Do all the teams face these types of unexpected situations, or are we special?

As the possessed ghost hunters advanced, adrenaline surged through my body. My hands steadied, and my focus sharpened. It's funny how everything else falls away in moments of extreme stress. All my doubts, fears, and exhaustion faded into the background. All that mattered was survival.

I thought about Korbin and Calvin, probably still in their meeting, blissfully unaware of the shit we'd walked into. Part of me was angry. Why weren't they here? Why did it always seem to fall on us to handle these insane situations? Another part of me was glad they weren't here. At least if things went south, the team would still have leadership.

As I stood there, guns trained on the approaching threats, a million thoughts raced through my mind. How do you fight something that's possessing a human body? Can bullets hurt spirits? What if we can't save the ghost hunters? The weight of these questions pressed down on me, making it hard to breathe.

I thought about my life before all this—my family, friends, and dreams. It all seemed so distant now, like a half-remembered dream. I wondered if I'd ever be able to go back to that life or if I was forever changed by what I'd seen and done. Part of me mourned for the innocence I'd lost, the normal life I'd never have again.

Another part of me that grew stronger each day embraced

this new reality. Yes, it was terrifying. Yes, it was dangerous. It was also exhilarating. I was making a difference, facing down evil in a way I never thought possible. Despite the fear and uncertainty, I felt alive in a way I never had before.

If we're going to bare our inner reflections... Things were much simpler in the old days. A little seduction, a dash of soul-stealing, and voilà— problem solved. Now I'm stuck watching this circus unfold, powerless to do anything but offer snarky commentary you largely ignore.

I suppose I should be grateful for the entertainment. It's more exciting than watching you study or listening to your inane conversations with your teammates. Still, the indignity grates on my nerves like sandpaper on a sunburn.

As the possessed ghost hunters closed in, I took a deep breath and steadied myself. I might not have signed up for this, but I'm here now, and I'll be damned if I go down without a fight. Whatever happens next, I have Damian at my back, Pandora in my head, and a strength inside me I'm only beginning to understand.

I was rooting for you and Damian. Not because I care, mind you. If you had failed, I'd be stuck in this body with no one to annoy. The priest looked like he was about to wet himself, by the way.

So bring it on, you possessed bastards. Katie's ready for a fight.

Let's hope we survive this farce. We probably will since the universe isn't done torturing me yet. Wake me up when there's a real challenge, like convincing you to wear something that doesn't look like it came from a thrift store clearance rack.

CHAPTER FOUR

Katie's Journal

That run-of-the-mill spirit call with Damian? Yeah, it turned into a full-blown haunted house nightmare. And not the fun kind with cheap jump scares and actors in masks. No, this was the real fucking deal.

I knew something was off when we stepped into that decrepit old building. The air felt thick, almost oppressive, and the eerie silence made the hair on the back of my neck stand up. But being the tough-as-nails badass I am, or at least pretend to be, I pushed those feelings aside and focused on the task at hand.

Please. I knew something was off right away. You took way too long to clue in.

That was when the whispers started. At first, I thought I was imagining things—you know, my mind playing tricks on me in a creepy old house. Then Damian heard them too, and suddenly they were everywhere. Disembodied voices giggling and whispering from every direction, bouncing off the walls like we were trapped in some fucked-up echo chamber.

Ha! I've seen more intimidating displays from drunken frat boys trying to impress sorority girls.

I'll admit it. For a split second, I felt a twinge of fear. I quickly squashed that shit down. Katie doesn't do fear, especially not when it comes to some punk-ass spirits trying to scare us. So I did what I do best. I got snarky.

"What's next, clowns? Fucking clowns? Red Rum? Men in masks with chainsaws?" I remember saying, my voice dripping with sarcasm. "The Kool-Aid man?"

Damian played along, bless his priestly heart. "Did you think those writers came up with all that stuff on their own?" he shouted over the laughter. "Except the Kool-Aid man. I loved him as a kid."

I chuckled at that. Leave it to Damian to find humor in a situation like this. My amusement was short-lived because that's when things really went off the rails.

The fucking *house* started laughing. Not just creepy giggles or whispers but full-on, deep-bellied laughter that morphed into the high-pitched squeals of children. I've seen some weird shit in my time with the Damned, but this was a whole new level of fucked up.

That was interesting. I admit, even I was a bit impressed. It's not every day you see a structure with a sense of humor. Predictably, you freaked out.

Then came the blood. Fucking rivers of it, seeping through the ceiling and walls like some kind of twisted, demonic Rorschach test. I watched in horror as it dripped down the peeling wallpaper and formed puddles on the floor. Part of me wanted to reach out and touch it to prove to myself this wasn't some elaborate hallucination. The rational part of my brain—yes, I *do* have one—held me back.

Ah, the pièce de résistance. The blood. Oh, the blood. Dripping from the ceilings, oozing down the walls—it was like a menstrual Niagara Falls in there. I half expected you to faint like some Victorian damsel. Instead, you just stood there, slack-jawed and wide-eyed. Amateur.

I turned to Damian, hoping he'd have an explanation or better yet, a way to make it all stop. His expression told me everything I needed to know. We were in uncharted territory.

"Have you been in this situation before?" I tried to keep the tremor out of my voice.

His response didn't exactly fill me with confidence. "This particular one? No, not exactly. I have to say, though, everything is textbook so far...just not the textbook I thought I would be teaching you from today."

Great. Just fucking great. We were dealing with some next-level demonic shit, and even our resident expert was flying blind. Damian tried to spin it as a learning experience. "Learning comes from being pulled into the situation, right?"

I wanted to smack him. "I am dead serious when I tell you I would have gladly taken a video tutorial on this one, Damian," I snapped. "I am pretty sure you didn't have to submerge me. The textbook case would have terrified me out of my mind."

But there was no time to argue about teaching methods because that's when the demon showed up. And let me tell you, this wasn't your garden-variety hellspawn. This fucker was massive, with a face that looked like it had been through a meat grinder and got put back together by a drunk toddler.

I'll give myself credit. My training kicked in, and I dodged its first attack. But as I crouched there, trying to get a clear shot, I realized how outmatched we were. This thing was built like a tank, and our bullets did little more than piss it off.

Apparently, this little horror show needed more players. That hulking brute had anger management issues. Your pathetic attempt to take it down was like watching a chihuahua try to fellate an elephant. Futile and disturbing.

For the record, Damian's little cross trick would have been about as effective as trying to stop a tsunami with a cocktail umbrella.

Things went from bad to worse when it grabbed Damian by the throat. I've never felt so helpless in my life, watching that monster dangle my partner like a ragdoll. I wanted to shoot, but I couldn't risk hitting Damian. All I could do was yell, "Put him down! Now!"

In retrospect, maybe antagonizing the demon wasn't the smartest move. It responded by hurling Damian at me like a human projectile. We went down in a tangle of limbs, and for a moment, all I could think was, "This is how I die—crushed by a priest in a haunted house. Fan-fucking-tastic."

Somehow, we got to our feet and fought back. We managed to wound the bastard, but that only made it angrier. As we chased it through the house, I thought about how absurd this situation was.

"How do I get myself into this shit?" I muttered as we pursued the demon. Part of me wanted to laugh hysterically at the sheer insanity of it all, but I knew if I started, I might not stop.

The so-called pursuit through the house was a comedy of errors. You and Damian bumbled around like drunken ballerinas while this demon —who missed the memo about being wounded—led you on a merry chase. It was like watching the world's most incompetent game of cat and mouse.

When we finally cornered it in the living room, I thought we had a chance. Then the fucker started growing. I'm not talking about a little growth spurt. This thing sprouted muscles where muscles had no business being. It was like watching a body-builder on fast-forward and steroids.

Ah, yes, the moment you and Damian, the dynamic duo, thought you were about to win. Bless your heart. As for the demon's transformation, I've seen better body modifications in back-alley Tijuana clinics. You two looked like you were watching Jesus rise from the dead.

As Damian and I huddled behind a dilapidated couch, trying to come up with a plan, I reflected that this was not how I expected my day to go. I signed up to fight evil, sure, but this? This was some next-level bullshit.

"We could run," Damian suggested, and for a moment, I was tempted. Then I thought about what would happen if we let this thing loose in the city. The carnage, the panic, the inevitable news coverage—*Demon on Steroids Terrorizes Las Vegas Strip*. Yeah, that wasn't an option.

Your little pow-wow behind the couch was the cherry on top of this shit sundae. Discussing running away like scared little children. Where's your bravado now, Katie dear? Where's that cocky attitude you love to parade around?

So there we were, outgunned and outmatched, facing down a demon that looked like it could bench press a bus. And Damian, in all his infinite wisdom, chose that moment to tell me he forgot to turn on our earpieces. I laughed. Because really, what else could I do?

Oh, Damian. Forgetting to turn on the earpieces? I've seen more compe-

tent leadership from drunken frat boys planning a keg party. It's a wonder you two can tie your shoelaces, let alone hunt demons.

As we sat there, backs against the couch, listening to the demon roar and grow larger, I wondered how the hell I ended up here. Not just in this house but in this life. Fighting demons, working with a priest who thinks this qualifies as a "date," and facing down creatures that shouldn't exist outside of nightmares.

I marveled at the sheer incompetence on display. If this is the best humanity can offer against the forces of darkness, well...let's just say I might be backing the wrong horse.

But who knows? Maybe you two idiots will pull off a miracle. Stranger things have happened. I once saw Caligula show mercy, after all. But I won't hold my breath. For now, I'll sit back and enjoy this little situation. It's not often you get front-row seats to such a spectacular shitshow.

But you know what? As terrified and pissed off as I was, there was a part of me that felt alive. More alive than I'd ever felt before. The adrenaline coursing through my veins, the weight of my gun in my hand, the knowledge that I was one of the few people standing between this monster and the unsuspecting world outside were exhilarating.

Don't get me wrong, I was still scared shitless. But there was also a thrill to it all, a sense of purpose I'd never experienced before joining the Damned. As I sat there, trying to come up with a plan to take down a demon that could probably use us as toothpicks, I realized something.

This is who I am now. This is what I do. I fight the monsters that most people don't even know exist. And yeah, it's terrifying and dangerous and completely insane, but it's also important. It matters.

So when Damian turned to me with a look that said he had an idea, but I probably wasn't going to like it, I knew I was in. Whatever crazy, half-baked plan he cooked up, I was ready to follow him into the fire. Because that's what partners do, right?

My body aches from bruises I didn't know I had, and I wonder what's next. More demons? Ghosts? Maybe a vampire or two for variety? Whatever it is, it won't be boring.

And you know what? I wouldn't have it any other way. Because as much as I bitch and moan about the danger and the insanity of it all, the truth is, I've never felt more like myself than I do right now.

So bring it on, universe. Throw your worst at me because Katie's ready for anything—even a steroid-pumped demon with anger management issues.

Let's hope I survive whatever Damian's cooking up in his crazy head.

CHAPTER FIVE

Pandora's Journal

Another day, another demonic dance with death. I swear, being trapped inside Katie's mortal meat suit is like being stuck in purgatory with a bunch of incompetent cherubs. But today? Today was different. Today, I got to stretch my demonic wings and show these pathetic humans what real power looks like.

It all started when that idiot Damian thought Katie's demon—that's me, you dimwit—would give her an edge against the big bad demon in the haunted house. Oh, if only he knew. I've been itching for a good fight since I got shoved into this flesh prison, and finally, the opportunity presented itself.

Katie, bless her naïve little heart, decided to "let me take over." As if she had a choice. I've been waiting for this moment, watching from the sidelines as she fumbled through life like a newborn fawn on ice. But when that guttural voice sang out, "Come out, come out, wherever you are!" I knew it was showtime.

I'm still not sure it was the right decision. I mean, other than the time with Garrett's demon, I've been trying to keep you at bay. Talk about a Hail Mary pass.

I remember leaning back on that musty old couch, trying to psych myself up for what I was about to do. Damian was clueless. Poor bastard had no idea what he was about to witness. I almost felt bad for him.

"I guess I don't have a choice," I said, more to myself than to him. "At least let me calm down and get my wits about me before calling in the team."
Damian started to ask why, but I shut him down. "Don't ask questions. It's better that way." If only he knew.
As I closed my eyes, I thought about how fucked up my life had become. I'd already lost my old life. Part of me wondered if letting this demon end it all would be better. At least I'd go out saving Damian's ass in the process. Heroic death and all that jazz.

Then I heard that guttural voice singing out, "Come out, come out, wherever you are!" and I knew I couldn't just roll over and die. Not like this. Not to this asshole.

So, I did it. I reached out in my mind. God, I hate how natural that's starting to feel.

"All right, Pandora. I know you've been watching this."

Your response was...well, pure Pandora. "Have I been watching that? That motherfucker! I know his ass all too well."

I swear, sometimes you enjoy this shit a little too much. I pushed on anyway. "I need your help."

You growled, "There's nothing I can enhance right now that will help you. He's a fucking killer. I'm the only one in the house who could kick his ass."

Well, no shit. That's why I was asking, you demonic drama queen. I kept my cool. "I know. If I let you take over for this, you have to promise to give my body back to me when you are done or Damian will kill us both."
"Understood. You'll get your body back."
I took a deep breath. "All right. Go for it."

I took control of Katie's body, relishing the feeling of power coursing through her veins. It was like slipping into a perfectly tailored suit if that suit were made of flesh and bone. I felt Damian's eyes on me. His jaw was practically on the floor. Amateur.

I laughed as I faced off against the demon. This bastard thought he was hot shit, but he was about to get a rude awakening. I screamed, "BASTARD! Killing is MY business!" It felt so good to use my voice again, even if it came from Katie's vocal cords.

Holy fuck. It was like being strapped into the world's most terrifying roller coaster. I felt my body shake and my muscles tense. I gritted my teeth so hard I thought they might shatter. Then my eyes shot open, and everything changed.

I could see through my eyes, but I had no control. It was like watching a movie from inside the main character's head. You stood, using my body like a puppet, and faced down that demon without a hint of fear.

When you screamed at him, I swore I felt my vocal cords vibrating with two distinct voices.

The fight that ensued was glorious. I used Katie's body like a finely tuned instrument, leaping through the air, emptying magazines into that fucker's face, and slashing him with my newly acquired demon claws. The look of recognition in his eyes when he realized who he was dealing with? Priceless.

I have to admit, it felt damn good to let loose. Katie's been keeping me on a tight leash, but now? I got to play. And play I did. I rode that demon like a mechanical bull at a trashy country bar, laughing my ass off the whole time. "Yee-haw. Ride 'em, cowbitch!" I taunted. God, I've missed this.

Poor Damian. I caught a glimpse of him during the fight, and he looked like his brain was about to short-circuit. Can't say I blame him. It's not every day you see your partner turn into a demon-possessed killing machine.

You loved every second of mayhem. Don't think I didn't know you smirked at the demon, practically daring him to come at her. "Oh, come now," you taunted. "You don't know an old friend when you see one? That's soooo disappointing."

The demon's reaction was...interesting. "You!" he hissed. "You were supposed to be gone!"

You just laughed, jumped onto his back, and dug those claws in deep while you cackled.

The fight wasn't without its challenges. That asshole threw me into a bookshelf, and let me tell you, the stench of decay in this house is worse than the ninth circle of Hell on taco night. But I got up, cracked my neck, and got ready for round two.

Talk about the world's most fucked-up rodeo. You laughed it off and wiped blood from my lips. Your "Oh, that reeks!" comment about the bookshelf was spot-on, though.

I couldn't resist taunting him a bit more. "So you want to play games," I said, using Katie's voice like a ventriloquist's dummy. "You didn't want to play games when there was the time or need to play them, and now—here in this old disgusting house—all you can come up with is bleeding walls. They are shaking their heads at you below."

The demon snarled, "You don't know anything. You're just jealous because you are stuck in that pathetic human body."

Jealous? As if. Being in Katie is far better than playing some B-movie reject like this asshole. I laughed and told him as much right before I launched myself at him again. "I'd rather be stuck in her than out here playing poltergeist. And I'd much rather be in her when I kill you and send you back to the flames!"

The fight was intense, I'll give him that. He threw me around like a rag doll, and Katie's body took a beating. But pain? Pain is just weakness leaving the body, and I was determined to make this demon leave his body in the most painful way possible.

Feeling the bricks hit my back as we crashed into the fireplace made me think, "This might be it. Game over."

I grabbed a fireplace poker and decided to end this little dance. I hissed, "The problem with you is that you don't know when to back off. You never *did* know how to back off. You always pushed the envelope, going just a bit too far."

"This game is boring me," he growled, eyeing me and moving a bit to his left.

"Me too." I jammed the poker into the floor handle first. It stood vertical, sharp end up.

In a move that would make even the most seasoned WWE wrestler proud, I lifted that demon over my head and impaled him on the fireplace poker. The sound of his flesh tearing and his screams? Music to my ears. I couldn't resist twisting the knife—or in this case, the poker—a little more.

My teeth clenched as you turned toward the upright poker. A dark smile spread across my face—your smile, not mine—as you slammed the demon down onto the spike, impaling him through the chest.

The demon's scream was...well, it's going to haunt my nightmares for a long time. You weren't done, though. You put my foot on his stomach and twisted, grinding him further onto the spike.

I whispered, letting my true voice flow through Katie's mouth, "Tell T'Chezz that I'll be coming for him. *And I will not be nice.*" I pressed my hand into his chest, channeling all my demonic energy into turning him into dust. The resulting explosion was more satisfying than a thousand orgasms.

As the dust settled, I didn't hide my pride. "This house is *clear*," I announced, feeling like a demonic version of that kid from *Poltergeist*. "Now that his stench is out, I can take a breath." I was ready to take on the world, maybe find a few more demons to obliterate, but Katie had other plans.

She started nagging me to give her body back. Can you believe the nerve? I just saved her ass, and she couldn't even give me five minutes to bask in the afterglow of demonic destruction. Fine, whatever. I reluctantly relinquished control, but not before making sure Damian knew who the real badass was.

A deal's a deal, even with a demon.

As I retreated to the back of Katie's mind, I couldn't help but feel a twinge of...something. Regret? Longing? Nah, it's probably indigestion from all the demon dust I inhaled. But I have to admit, it felt good to be out there again, to feel the rush of battle and the thrill of victory.

This little adventure has only whetted my appetite for more. Katie might think she's in control, but I'm always here, waiting for my next chance to shine. And when that chance comes? Well, let's just say the demons of this world better watch their backs. Because Pandora's box has been opened, and I'm ready to raise some hell.

My body went limp, and suddenly I was back in control. It was like waking up from the world's worst hangover, multiplied by about a thousand.

Damian caught me before I hit the floor. Poor guy looked like he'd seen a ghost—or, well, a demon, I guess. "Katie?" he asked, his voice shaky.

"It's me," I croaked. Everything hurt. "I think so. Though I have to say, I never want to hit a brick fireplace at that speed ever again. I don't know why I don't have broken bones."

Damian helped me to the couch, promising to check me out when we got back. "I've never seen anything like that before," he said.

I chuckled, even though it made my ribs ache. "Yeah, me either. I could see everything she was doing and feel everything my body went through, but I couldn't do anything. It was the strangest feeling."

As I stood, I noticed the cut on my arm was already healing. Damian noticed too, but I pulled down my sleeve. No need to freak him out more than he already was.

We talked a bit more about what had happened, about how rare demons like that were. I picked up a small piece of brick as a souvenir, ignoring your snarky suggestion to take the poker instead.

Now, hours later, I'm still trying to process it all. The fight, the possession, the things you said...especially that bit about T'Chezz. When I asked you about it later, you brushed it off. "Nobody important. At least not yet."

I don't buy it for a second. There's more going on here, and I'm going to figure it out. For now, I need sleep. My body feels like it's been through a war, and my mind isn't far behind.

One thing's for sure. Life with you will never be boring. God help me.

CHAPTER SIX

I'm still trying to wrap my head around everything that happened with the ghost hunters and that haunted house. I mean, I knew being Damned came with its share of weird experiences, but that? It took the cake.

Blah, blah, blah. Get over the angst already, sweetheart. I swear, being in your head is like being stuck in a never-ending episode of The Twilight Zone, *except with more demons and less Rod Serling.*

Letting Pandora out to handle things was... God, it's so fucked up to even think it. I *asked* the demon inside me to take control. How's that for a mindfuck?

If you'd let me take over more often, we could really make some waves in this demon-hunting business. But no...you had to be Little Miss Perfect and play by the rules. Rules! As if demons give a shit about rules.

*It's like trying to teach table manners to Attila the Hun. Utterly
pointless.*

When I came back to myself, Damian was hiding behind a
couch. A couch! Mr. Tough Guy, cowering like a scared kid. I
would've laughed if I wasn't so freaked out. The ghost hunters
were all passed out on the floor with demons inside them.

Damian looked at me like he'd seen a ghost. I guess he had, in
a way. He was terrified of me—or rather, of Pandora. Can't say I
blame him. I'm pretty terrified of her too. The kicker is he
decided not to tell anyone about what happened. About me.
About Pandora.

Part of me is relieved. I mean, I don't want to be suspended or
worse. Another part of me is pissed. This is who I am now,
whether I like it or not. Hiding it feels wrong. Like I'm ashamed
of myself. Fuck that noise. I didn't ask for any of this.

Damian called Derek to report in, and I could tell he was
dancing around the truth. It was almost funny watching him try
to find the right words. Almost. If it wasn't my ass on the line, I
might have enjoyed his discomfort more.

*Ha! Damian covering for us was almost entertaining. He was about as
subtle as Julius Caesar on the Ides of March. "Nothing to say right
now." Smooth, real smooth. I'm surprised he didn't blurt, "Hey, Derek!
Guess what? Katie has a demon inside her, and it's not me!"*

Then he dropped another bomb on me. We have recruits. One
"medium rare," whatever the fuck that means, and one "rare."
Turns out "rare" means not infected. Can you believe that?
Someone willingly signing up for this shitshow without being
Damned? Talk about a glutton for punishment.

Damian tried to explain it to me, asking how I'd feel if I could
return to my old life but keep my memories. You know what?

He's right. I couldn't go back. Not now, not ever. This life is part of me now for better or worse.

Such an enlightening conversation. Medium rare and rare, indeed. Might as well be discussing a fucking steakhouse menu instead of potential team members. Bless your naïve little heart for not understanding the reference at first. I sometimes wonder how you survived this long without me.

What really frosted me was Damian talking about not revealing your "multiple personalities." Multiple personalities, my ass. I'm not some figment of his imagination or a result of trauma. I'm a full-fledged, card-carrying succubus, thank you very much. The audacity of reducing me to a personality disorder is insulting.

Enough about the newbies. We had to deal with the ghost hunters. By "we," I mean me. Damian told me I had to exorcise the demons from them. No pressure or anything, right? Just casually perform multiple exorcisms like it's no big deal. Sometimes I wonder if Damian forgets I'm still new to all this.

I did it, though. I fucking did it. Let me tell you, it was not pleasant. It felt like reaching into someone's soul and ripping out a parasite. I guess that was pretty much what I did. The ghost hunters woke up with killer headaches and no memory of what happened. Lucky bastards.

You want to know the really fucked up part? They were disappointed. Disappointed! We saved their asses from being demon puppets, and they were upset because they missed out on some "career-making" footage. I swear, some people have no sense of self-preservation.

I tried to be understanding. I really did. But when Brad started whining about how they're "professionals" and "scientists" who don't get invited to the party, I nearly lost it. Give me a fucking break. You want to talk about being outcasts? Try having a demon inside you that can take over your body at any moment. Then we'll talk about not being invited to the party.

That conversation was particularly grating. Those idiots were more concerned about their equipment and missed opportunities than the fact that they nearly became demon chow. Can you say, "Chickens complaining about missed photo ops with the fox?"

Don't even get me started on their "professionalism." Scientists, my perfectly sculpted ass. They were about as scientific as a medieval witch hunt. If they had any real understanding of the supernatural world, they wouldn't have gotten themselves into that mess in the first place.

Outcasts? As if we had anything in common with those bumbling amateurs. We're not outcasts. We're fucking rock stars in the demon-hunting world. They should have kissed the ground we walked on.

Damian smoothed things over, explaining why we couldn't let them keep their demon buddies for the sake of research. He's good at the diplomatic bullshit. Me? I'm more of a "tell it like it is" kind of girl. Probably why I'm not in charge.

Then they asked if I helped. Damian lied through his teeth, saying it was my first time dealing with spirits and I was only there to observe. Part of me wanted to scream, "Actually, I'm the one who saved all your asses!" I kept my mouth shut. Go me.

Ha! If by "observe," he meant "saved all your sorry asses," then sure, that was exactly what happened.

After the ghost hunters left, Damian and I had a moment to breathe. Then he dropped another bombshell on me. The demon I took out? Worth twenty-five thousand dollars. Twenty-five fucking thousand! And because we're keeping my little Pandora situation under wraps, I can't claim the bounty.

Damian offered me the money anyway, but it didn't feel right. He's the one who brought us there, who's covering for me. But he insists. Says he couldn't accept it knowing he spent the whole time hiding behind a musty old couch. Fair point, I guess.

That payday could have set us up nicely. But nooooo...Little Miss Goody-Goody played it safe. I could have bought so many new outfits with that money. Or, you know, saved it for a rainy day or whatever responsible thing you would have done with it.

The cherry on top of the shit sundae was Damian's offer to give you the money for the job. On the one hand, it's about damn time someone recognized our value. On the other hand, it's infuriating that we have to hide our true potential. We could be ruling this demon-hunting gig, but instead, we're playing second fiddle to Mr. Constipation and his merry band of misfits.

We ended up going to the pub for a drink and some food. It was nice. Normal, even. I felt like a person again for a while, not some freak with a demon inside her. Damian and I talked and laughed like two regular people after a long day at work. If our work involved exorcising demons and lying to ghost hunters, that is.

How delightfully mundane after all the drama and excitement. I suppose I should have been grateful for the brief respite from the insanity, but part of me itched for more action. More chances to show what we're capable of. Enjoy the illusion that everything will be okay, you poor, sweet, naïve girl. If you only knew what's in store for us.

I could tell Damian was trying to show me everything would be okay. For a moment, I almost believed it. Then reality crashed back in with a phone call. Korbin called a meeting. Everyone back ASAP.

Sigh. Just when I started to enjoy, or at least tolerate the calm. Heaven forbid we have more than five minutes of peace in this godforsaken job. Fantastic. Another meeting, better known as another opportunity to sit around and pretend you're not harboring a kickass succubus inside you.

So here I am. My head is spinning, my emotions are all over the place, and I have no idea what will happen next. Will Damian keep my secret? Will Pandora make another appearance? What about these recruits?

One thing's for sure. This job is never boring. Terrifying, confusing, and occasionally nauseating? Absolutely. But never boring.

Side note: I don't want to see the view inside a demon's lair or something equally fucked up. But with my luck? No promises.

What fresh hell awaits us at this meeting? Recruits to babysit? More demons to exorcise while hiding our true potential? Or perhaps an opportunity to finally show these mortals what we're truly made of.

I guess I should stop brooding. We need to get back for the meeting. I have a message for my dear inner demon.

Pandora, I know you can hear me. You might think you're hot shit, but remember this. I'm the one in control. This is my body, my life. You're along for the ride. So don't get any ideas about taking over again. Because next time, I might not be so nice about taking back control.

It's so cute that you think you're in control. I'm biding my time, letting you believe that. I'll take control when you inevitably falter. Because let's face it, in this world of demons and danger, sometimes you need a little evil to do a whole lot of good.

Meanwhile, may our adventures be plentiful, our enemies vanquished, and our true nature deliciously hidden. For now.

CHAPTER SEVEN

What a fucking day. I thought I'd seen it all, but the universe had other plans. Just when I thought things were settling into some semblance of normalcy, if you can call our demon-hunting lifestyle "normal," we got two recruits. Great. More testosterone to deal with.

Another fucking day in paradise, trapped inside a walking disaster. If I had known being a succubus meant playing second fiddle to a human with the emotional range of a teaspoon, I'd have chosen a different career path. Maybe I should've been a lawyer instead—then I'd be surrounded by my kind.

Let me back up. Korbin called a team meeting today, and I could tell something was up. He had that look in his eye, you know? The one that says, "Brace yourselves, shit's about to get real." And boy, did it ever.

First, he thanked Damian, Derek, and me for "holding down

the fort" while they were gone. I exchanged glances with Damian, and I swear I felt the electricity between us. Derek noticed, of course. Nothing gets past that guy. I'll have to be more careful.

The clusterfuck began with Korbin gathering the team like some discount Captain America. He thanked you, Damian, and Derek for "holding down the fort." Please. As if you could hold down anything more substantial than a paper napkin in a light breeze.

Then came the news. Two new team members. Because we needed more people to witness my slow descent into madness. Joy.

First up was Eric, the medical guy. Ex-military, special ops trained. He stood, all confident and shit, and dropped the bomb that he's a volunteer. Can you believe that? This guy willingly signed up for this hellscape. Either he's the bravest son of a bitch I've ever met, or he's completely off his rocker.

When Damian asked why he volunteered—beating me to the punch, damn him—Eric's story nearly knocked me on my ass. He talked about his team getting ambushed by a coven of Damned. Two of his buddies were torn apart right in front of him. Jesus Christ. I've seen some fucked up shit, but that's a whole new level of horror.

The way he described his friend Anthony getting possessed sent chills down my spine. I wondered if that's what I look like when Pandora takes over. The thought made me sick to my stomach.

Eric's anger was palpable. He wants revenge, retribution for his friends. Part of me admires his dedication, but another part wants to shake him and scream, "Run, you idiot! Get out while you still can!" I guess it's too late for that now. He's in it for the long haul, just like the rest of us poor bastards.

He spun quite a sob story. Boo-hoo. Welcome to the club, buddy. We all have our trauma porn to share. But no, this masochist volunteered for this shitshow. Blender, meet finger. Don't act surprised when you lose your appendage.

Then there's Jeremy, the ex-FBI guy. His story was equally fucked up. A sting operation gone horribly wrong, ending with demons and carnage. Two dead, two infected, including Jeremy. His partner is on life support with no real future ahead of him. Moments like these make me realize how lucky, if you can call it that, I am to have Pandora. At least I'm still functional, still fighting.

Another tale of woe. These humans and their petty little lives. It's almost adorable how they think their suffering is unique. News flash—the world's been going to Hell in a handbasket since Caligula decided togas were too restrictive for his orgies.

I tried to welcome them both, spouting some bullshit about us being a family and that I hoped they loved it like I do. But with fewer socks lying around the place. The family part is true, in a way. We're all we've got in this godforsaken world. But as I said it, I felt like a fraud. How can I talk about family when I'm harboring a demon inside me? When I'm keeping secrets that could tear us all apart?

Bless your vapid little heart for that "welcome to the 'family.'" Although it's more like a dysfunctional circus troupe with a death wish. As for your comment about fewer socks lying around? Sweetheart, with two more testosterone-fueled meatheads in the mix, you'll be drowning in dirty laundry faster than you can say "toxic masculinity."

After the meeting, everyone dispersed to the living area. Korbin pulled Damian aside for a debrief about the "house issue" from earlier. My stomach churned. What would Damian tell him? We both know the truth would be too much, but lying to Korbin doesn't sit right with me.

A "debrief," AKA code for "I know you're hiding shit. Spill it." I would've loved to be a fly on the wall for that conversation. Damian, the cryptic bastard, probably danced around the truth like it was a maypole.

I retreated to my room, using the excuse of an Amazon package as a cover. Pandora was more interested in her damn game show. Sometimes I envy her ability to disconnect from all this madness.

Because we need more useless crap in this hellhole. And you interrupted my game show viewing with it! At least you recorded the program for me. Small mercies, I suppose.

I wonder what Damian and Korbin are discussing. Part of me wants to march down there and tell Korbin everything—about Pandora, what happened at the house, all of it. I know I can't. It would put everyone at risk, and as much as I hate to admit it, we need this team intact to have any chance of surviving what's coming.

I overheard Derek talking to Jeremy about me before I left. I'm supposed to be the "glue" that holds this team together. Derek called me "granite with a heart." It's flattering, I guess, but it also terrifies me. How can I be the foundation when I'm barely holding myself together most days?

Jeremy was skeptical and couldn't fathom how you could be the "glue" holding everything together. Oh, the poor bastard. If he only knew. You're not glue. You're more like duct tape—versatile, a bit tacky, and prone to leaving a mess when someone tries to remove you.

Derek comparing you to granite made me laugh. You're not an immov-

able force of nature. Play-Doh would be more accurate. Easily moldable and dries out if left exposed for too long.

The weight of it all is crushing sometimes. Being the only woman on the team, harboring a demon, and trying to maintain some semblance of normalcy while fighting literal hellspawn...it's a lot. With these new guys here now, I feel like I'm under even more scrutiny. Will they see through my façade? Will they realize what I am?

I can't stop thinking about what Eric and Jeremy have been through. Their stories are horrific, but in a way, I envy their clarity. They know exactly why they're here and what they're fighting for. Me? I'm still trying to figure out if I'm more human or demon most days.

Pandora's been unusually quiet tonight. I think even she can sense the shift in dynamics. Or maybe she's sulking because I made her record her precious game show. Either way, the silence in my head is a relief but unsettling.

I wonder what tomorrow will bring. Will we be sent on another mission? Will I have to pretend to be normal around Eric and Jeremy? Will Damian and I get a moment alone to discuss what happened at the house?

God, Damian. Thinking about him makes my heart race. The way he looked at me today, during the meeting and after... There's something there, something dangerous and exhilarating. I can't let myself go down that road. It's too risky for both of us.

It's almost impressive how you humans dance around the truth. You're all so afraid of facing reality that you'd rather create elaborate fantasies than admit you're in over your heads.

I should try to get some sleep. Who knows what fresh hell awaits us tomorrow? But before I do, I need to make a plan. I need to figure out how to navigate this new dynamic and keep my secret while still being the "granite" this team needs.

Maybe I'll start by unpacking that Amazon box. Might as well have some new socks to go with all this new baggage, right?

Fuck, I miss the days when my biggest worry was passing my college exams. Now I'm worried about passing as a human. Life's a bitch, then you get possessed by one.

I'm a silent observer in this carnival of idiocy. Sometimes I wonder if I'm being punished for some cosmic transgression. Did I piss off a god in a past life? Maybe I accidentally stepped on Buddha's toe or gave Zeus the finger.

Whatever the reason, I'm trapped and surrounded by humans who couldn't find their asses with both hands and a map. It's enough to make a succubus consider celibacy. Almost.

Here's hoping tomorrow brings fewer demons and more answers. Who am I kidding? In this line of work, it's always more demons.

Note to self: Find out what kind of game shows Pandora likes. Might come in handy as a bargaining chip someday. Or, you know, for those moments when I need her to shut up so I can think straight. A girl can dream, right?

Another day, another dollar, as these meatbags like to say. Tomorrow will bring new challenges, idiocies, and undoubtedly new ways for Katie to test the limits of my patience. Until then, I'll be here, plotting my escape and dreaming of the day when I can finally spread my wings and fly far, far away from this cesspool of human incompetence.

CHAPTER EIGHT

Another day in the life of a demon hunter. Korbin gave us a "free day" to bond with the new guys before diving into training. How thoughtful of him. I spent some time training with Derek in the pit, which was pretty nice. It's always good to work out the kinks and keep our skills sharp.

By dinner time, we were all ready to hit the bar. Korbin and Damian led our merry band of misfits through the back alleys of Vegas to our favorite dive bar. This place is like a second home to us—rough, wild, and perfect for our crew.

Team bonding. How quaint. As if forced socialization will magically transform this ragtag group of misfits into a cohesive unit. I'd sooner expect Caligula to host a successful temperance meeting.

The siren call of alcohol proved too strong to resist. Off we traipsed through the back alleys of Vegas like a parade of drunken lemmings.

You should have seen Eric's and Jeremy's faces when we walked in. Their eyes were as big as saucers, taking in all the roughnecks arguing and fighting around us. I smirked. Welcome to our world, boys.

Korbin grabbed a table in the center of the room, which I knew was trouble waiting to happen. But hey, who am I to spoil the fun? We ordered food and drinks, and I settled in to watch the show unfold.

Eric, bless his heart, couldn't keep his mouth shut. He had to ask about the duct-taped furniture. I exchanged glances with the others, trying not to burst out laughing. Oh, sweet summer child. You'll learn soon enough.

As if your brief tenure with these buffoons grants you any real status or skills.

Sure enough, about twenty minutes later, all hell broke loose. Two women at a nearby table started screaming at each other. I swear, it's like clockwork in this place. I caught Damian's eye and immediately grabbed my food. No way was I letting my grilled cheese become collateral damage.

Seriously, the furniture should've given our fresh-faced yokels their first clue. But no, it took a full-blown catfight for reality to dawn on our fresh-faced newcomers. Two women, fueled by alcohol and misplaced aggression, decided to reenact a scene from Crouching Tiger, Hidden Dragon *in the middle of the bar.*

I leaned back, enjoying the show and feeling smug. For once, I wasn't the newbie. It was time for Eric and Jeremy to get a taste of what they'd signed up for.

Jeremy's face was priceless. He sat there with a French fry dangling from his lips as he watched these women go at it like trained fighters. I had to bite my lip to keep from laughing.

Calvin chimed in about how sexy it was. I rolled my eyes. Men.

I admit, watching Jeremy's face as he realized this wouldn't be a stereo-typical hair-pulling slap-fest was mildly amusing. Calvin calling it "sexy" was par for the course...because nothing says arousing quite like two inebriated women beating each other senseless over an inane argument.

I kept my eyes on Eric, waiting for him to catch on. Slowly, he raised his food basket, following our lead. Jeremy, on the other hand, remained blissfully oblivious. Oh, this was going to be good.

When the grand finale came, it was everything I'd hoped for. The larger woman picked up her smaller opponent, Faleena, and slammed her onto our table. Down went the duct-taped monstrosity, along with Jeremy's food. I joined in the chorus of "Olé!" that erupted from our group.

Poor Jeremy. He looked so confused, pulling his eyebrows together as he peered under the wreckage. Then Faleena crawled out, covered in ketchup and fries. I thought I was going to bust a gut trying not to laugh.

Don't think I didn't realize how eagerly you anticipated this. Including the bartender having a replacement table ready to go.

The best part? She handed Jeremy what was left of his food and apologized before heading back to sit with the woman who'd kicked her ass. The look on Jeremy's face was priceless.

"What the hell? Where did you people bring me?" he asked in confusion and awe.

Calvin raised his glass. "The finest establishment on the sandy coast. Welcome to Torn Asunder!"

We all joined in the toast, and I felt a sense of belonging. This crazy, messed-up group of people had become my family.

I shared Jeremy's bewilderment when the two combatants hugged it out and went back to their meal as if nothing had happened. What kind of twisted logic governs this place where violence is only a prelude to reconciliation?

The night went on, and Korbin regaled us with stories of Damian's first time at the bar. I have to admit, the mental image of our resident priest flying through the air after picking a fight with the biggest guy in the place was hilarious.

Because nothing says "elite demon-hunting squad" quite like reminiscing about drunken misadventures and priestly brawls. If I had eyes to roll, they'd be permanently stuck in the back of my head by now.

As we stumbled back to base that night, I had mixed emotions. On the one hand, I was glad to have some new blood in the group. On the other, I worried about whether they could handle what was coming. This life isn't for everyone, and I've seen too many good people broken by it.

The next morning came way too early. We all gathered in the training pit, and Calvin announced that Jeremy and I would be sparring. I felt Derek's eyes on me as Calvin explained the rules.

More idiocy disguised as training with Calvin as the ringmaster of this circus. Derek's muttered comment about pain tolerance was perhaps the only moment of clarity in this entire farce.

"I won't be too hard on him," I promised Derek, but he didn't look convinced.

"Uh-huh," he said. "Good intentions pave the road to hell."

As Jeremy and I stepped into the center of the pit, I felt his nerves radiating off him. It made me more confident, but I also felt a twinge of sympathy. I remembered what it was like to be the new kid, trying to prove yourself.

That rush of superiority was almost intoxicating.

Calvin gave Jeremy a once-over, and doubt showed in his eyes. Jeremy noticed too and shifted uncomfortably. I almost felt bad for him.

I stripped off my sweat jacket and tossed it to Derek, then stretched my arms over my head. I caught Jeremy eyeing me, probably thinking he had this in the bag because of his size advantage. Oh, honey. You have no idea what you're in for.

Pandora chuckled in my head. "Who the hell is this chump?"

"New guy," I replied silently. "We're going to take it easy on him. We don't want to hurt his ego too much."

"Right." Pandora sighed, and I could practically feel her eye roll.

Calvin patted Jeremy on the shoulder and said something about tenderizing new meat. I had to bite back a laugh at the look on Jeremy's face.

As we squared off, Jeremy was still distracted, looking at Calvin. Big mistake, buddy.

When Calvin yelled, "Go!" I stood there for a few seconds, giving Jeremy a chance to get his head in the game. He kept staring at Calvin like a deer in headlights. Well, if that's how he wanted to play it...

I crouched and launched into a kick that connected solidly with his head. I pulled it at the last second, not wanting to knock him out cold on his first day. Still, the impact was enough to send him to his hands and knees.

He was woefully unprepared. That kick nearly ended the fight before it began.

"Good one. Good one..." he mumbled, rubbing his face. "I guess you got to teach the new guy that there is no mer—"

I didn't let him finish. This wasn't about mercy. It was about survival. I swept his feet out from under him, sending him crashing to the mat again.

"Get up." I stood over him. "If I were a demon, you'd be dead, and your guts would be spilled all over the mat."

He groaned and pulled himself to his feet, eyeing me warily. The wheels were turning in his head, trying to figure out how to take me down. Part of me wanted to crush his ego completely, to show him exactly why I was an essential part of this team. I reined in that impulse. This was about training, not humiliation.

Jeremy lunged at me, but his movements were telegraphed so clearly I could have dodged them in my sleep. I easily sidestepped him, pushing his head as he passed.

"You're leading with your legs. I can tell which way you'll go and what you'll do because you move your legs first, then the rest of your body."

He tried again, and this time I grabbed his arm, pulled it behind his back, and simulated slitting his throat. "Like this." I stepped back. "I knew exactly where you were going, and I took you exactly where I wanted you to go. If you do that, the demons will notice, and you'll be their next meal in a heartbeat."

Jeremy grunted, frustration evident in his voice. "They don't have intelligence. They're big sacks of fucking meat."

I glanced at Damian, remembering all too well how wrong that assumption was. "Yeah, until they plan an attack on you and force your inner demon to fight. Anyway, you can't let them know what your plans are."

I could see the determination in Jeremy's eyes. He was tired of my "lessons," tired of feeling outmatched. He dug his back foot in, preparing to lunge at me with all his weight.

I almost felt bad for what I was about to do.

As he leapt toward me, I met him with a front snap-kick to

the chin. His eyes rolled back, and he crumpled to the mat, out cold.

I confess to a certain satisfaction in watching you dominate this match. Mind you, not out of any fondness for you, but rather the visceral pleasure of witnessing someone's inflated sense of self-worth being punctured so thoroughly. Jeremy's assumption that his size and FBI training would be enough to overcome your skill was deliciously misguided.

However, your attempts at instruction during the fight were almost comical. As if a few pointers about telegraphing moves would suddenly transform this bumbling oaf into a competent fighter.

When he came to, Calvin and I were standing over him. I tried to look concerned, but I couldn't quite keep the smirk off my face.

"So, would you tell me how the FBI uses the strategy of blocking a front snap-kick with your chin?" Calvin asked while helping Jeremy to his feet. "To be honest, it didn't really look like it worked out too well for you."

That sarcastic inquiry was perhaps the most entertaining moment of this mini-drama.

As Jeremy rubbed his chin and winced in pain, part of me felt satisfied. He needed to learn that size isn't everything in this line of work. Another part of me felt a twinge of guilt. We're supposed to be a team, after all.

I sighed and ran a hand through my hair. This job isn't easy, and it's not for everyone. Jeremy and Eric have a long road ahead if they want to survive in this world. I hope they're up for the challenge.

I wonder how long it will take before they realize what they signed up for. How long before they understand that fighting demons isn't only about physical strength but about mental forti-tude and the ability to face your inner darkness.

Only time will tell, I suppose. For now, all I can do is try to whip them into shape and hope they don't get themselves killed in the process. Just another day in the life of a demon hunter, right?

God, I need a drink.

Another day dealing with this purgatory of mediocrity. You humans with your petty squabbles and misguided attempts at camaraderie continue to astound me with your capacity for idiocy. Yet I'm inextri-cably drawn into your drama, an unwilling spectator to this tragi-comedy of errors.

And the day isn't over yet. Sigh. May the gods have mercy on my nonexistent soul.

CHAPTER NINE

My day wasn't done after kicking Jeremy's ass. I *almost* feel bad for the guy. He's got this whole macho act going on like he can't possibly lose to a girl. News flash, buddy. This girl laid you out flat. I had to help him up off the mat and apologize for knocking him out cold. Talk about a bruised ego.

I decided to give the new guys a break from my relentless ass-kicking and headed to the weight area. No need to completely demoralize them on day one, right? As I was pumping iron, Derek sauntered over with his shit-eating grin.

"How's it goin', Rambo?" He leaned over me like some creepy gym bro.

I rolled my eyes. "Oh, you know, just the usual. Kicking recruits' asses, trying not to die, and smashing the patriarchy one bench press at a time." I lowered my voice and added with a wink, "I'm *Batdamned...*"

Derek chuckled and said Korbin wanted to see me in his

office. Great. Just what I needed—a mysterious summons from the big boss. My stomach flipped, but I tried to play it cool.

"Any idea what he wants?" I tried to keep the nervousness out of my voice.

"Not a clue." Derek shrugged, utterly unhelpful as usual.

I grabbed my towel and water bottle, mentally preparing myself for whatever Korbin had in store. As I walked toward his office, I chatted with my favorite demonic roommate.

"Can you sense anything?" I asked Pandora silently.

"I can't tell what he wants to talk to you about," she replied. "But there's something different. I feel it getting stronger as we get closer to the office."

Fantastic. More supernatural weirdness. Pandora explained that a ward was blocking major powers from Korbin's office. It was a test to see who was dominant, me or the demon inside me. No pressure or anything.

Finally, someone with a modicum of sense! Not you—you went into panic mode, fretted about already feeling its effects, and asked if you should be ready for a fight. Oh, honey. If you only knew the fights I've been in. They make your little scuffles look like a toddler's tea party. Seriously, relax. Sometimes I wonder if I'm living inside a human or a bundle of anxiety wrapped in skin.

I stood outside Korbin's door with my hand hovering over the knob. Part of me wanted to turn tail and run, but I've never been one to back down from a challenge. I took a deep breath and knocked.

"Come in," Korbin called.

Here goes nothing, I thought, and stepped over the threshold. To my surprise and relief, I made it through without bursting into flames or turning into a toad. Small victories, right?

I told you the ward wouldn't be a problem, although I admit your luck is about as consistent as a politician's promises.

Korbin got right down to business, asking about my recent tumble during a spirit-handling gig. I brushed it off as only a few bumps and scratches. Nothing this badass can't handle. Then he dropped the real bombshell. He wanted to talk about my role on the team.

"Just a bump and some scratches. I heal pretty fast," you claimed. Yeah, thanks to me, sweetheart.

"With the newbies here Calvin is my second-in-command, and with Derek pretty much helping with everything else, that leaves you as my heavy," Korbin explained.

I raised an eyebrow. "Your heavy?"

He went on to divulge that I was basically the Jill-of-all-trades, the one who gets shit done, and a "major badass among the fighters." I'm not gonna lie. My ego swelled at that. Then he hit me with the real kicker. I'd be part of the decision-making process for weapons and defense.

Awww. My little host, all grown up and kicking ass. Yes, that's a teeny bit of pride.

Holy shit. This was big. Like, really big. I tried to play it cool, but inside I was doing a happy dance. Picking out sharp, explosive, and dangerous toys? Sign me up!

Play it cool? I'd laugh if I could. "It's like a damn dream come true," you gushed.

Korbin seemed pleased with my enthusiasm. He even joked about setting up volleyball tournaments at the compound. I had to laugh at that. If my old coach could see me now, she'd probably have a heart attack. Or maybe she'd finally be satisfied with my "ferocious" attitude.

Then came the bigger surprise. Korbin invited me to join him and Calvin at a weapons demonstration in Las Vegas in two days. It was like Christmas came early, but instead of presents under the tree, we would shop for high-tech gadgets of destruction. I was practically giddy with excitement.

There are times I think I'm living in a walking armory with a penchant for violence.

As I left Korbin's office, I couldn't resist throwing a little parting shot his way. "I'll always be stronger than my demon." I tapped the doorframe. Take that, weird office ward.

Oh, honey. Keep telling yourself that. One day, you might even believe it.

After all the excitement, I decided I'd had enough training for one day. I headed up to my room for a much-needed shower and some quality time with my favorite demonic frenemy.

"Check out this new bra," I told Pandora as I dressed. She's weirdly obsessed with lingerie, but I'm starting to see the appeal. There's something empowering about wearing kickass under-wear, even if no one else can see it.

Turns out you have taste in lingerie after all. Not that anyone would have known when you first got here.

I flopped onto my bed and flipped on the TV, ready for some mindless entertainment. Pandora was practically vibrating with excitement.

"Yessssss," she hissed. "Isn't *All of Our Lives* on first?"

I nodded, settling in for some ridiculous soap opera drama. "Yep. Lucas is coming out, and the maid is going to reveal that she's Antonio's real mother."

"I love this shit," Pandora said gleefully. "And *The Price Game* comes on afterward. You know how much I love that fucking game. Did you know you can write to them and get tickets? You should do that."

I had to laugh at her enthusiasm. "And do what if I'm chosen? Everyone thinks I'm dead. I can't just pop up on a game show."

"Shit," Pandora grumbled. "That's just my fucking luck. I could totally beat those idiots. I mean, I've been alive forever, so I have some good knowledge in my brain."

We bantered back and forth about her newfound obsessions, from fancy facial scrubs to specific scents. According to her, most demons aren't big on personal hygiene. I couldn't resist teasing her about becoming more "human."

You call it girliness and think my love for Lancôme facial scrubs, pleasant scents, and chocolate makes me feminine. Ha! Try living in the depths of Hell for millennia. You'd crave anything that doesn't smell like brimstone and despair too.

"Whatever," she huffed. "Men like lingerie too."

I rolled my eyes. "Yeah, men like taking *off* lingerie. And I don't mean those outliers who like to wear it, like that FBI guy in history...uh, whatshisname."

"Seriously?" Pandora asked, incredulous. "You humans had a person making decisions in the government whose name was Whatshisname?"

I groaned. "No, dammit. His name was J. Edgar Hoover. I just didn't want to be bothered with remembering."

A knock on the door interrupted our bizarre history lesson. It was Derek, inviting me to watch a movie with the rest of the team. They were screening *Priest,* a thriller-drama that's a comedy to our merry band of demon hunters. How's that for irony?

Oh, sweet summer child. To us demons, it's a comedy of errors.

I followed Derek to the common room, where everyone had gathered. Calvin lounged in the back like the cool kid in class while the newbies were front and center, probably hoping to impress. I chuckled at seeing our resident man of the cloth settling in to watch a movie about vampire-hunting priests.

"Why do I find it weird that the priest is here to watch *Priest*?" I smirked.

Damian winked. "From what I've heard, I could have been the main character."

Before we started the movie, I remembered my dad's special popcorn recipe. I jumped up to head to the kitchen, ignoring the chorus of groans behind me. Hey, if they wanted to complain, they could make their own damn snacks.

As I whipped up batch after batch of sugary blue goodness, much to Pandora's dismay—she wanted red, the bloodthirsty demon—nostalgia hit hard. My mom used to call it "fairy popcorn," saying it had a little magic in it. Looking around at my ragtag group of demon hunters, all with blue-stained fingers and grins on their faces, I realized that maybe there was still some magic left in the world after all.

Blue sugar-coated popcorn. How quaint. I suggested red, but that was too reminiscent of blood for you, our delicate little flower. As if you don't see enough of it in your line of work.

Predictably, the boys devoured the popcorn like ravenous hellhounds. By the end, you all looked like you'd feasted on Smurfs. Charming.

By the time we settled in to watch the movie, fingers sticky and bellies full of popcorn, I felt content. It's a rare feeling these days, with all the chaos and danger that comes with this life. While sitting there surrounded by people who have become my weird, demon-hunting family, I realized that maybe I'm exactly where I'm supposed to be.

You realize this is absurd, right? An ancient, powerful demon reduced to watching B-movie schlock with a bunch of humans who think they're hot shit because they can exorcise a few low-level imps.

Who would have thought a former college volleyball player would end up as the "heavy" for a team of supernatural ass-kickers? Life's funny like that, I guess. As the movie started and the guys cracked jokes about the inaccuracies, I smiled. Yeah, my life is always an unpredictable walk on the wild and crazy side. But you know what? I wouldn't have it any other way.

Tomorrow, I'll go back to training, kicking ass, and preparing for our little weapons shopping spree in Vegas. For tonight, I'll enjoy this moment of normalcy, or what passes for normal in our world. Cheers to staying alive and kicking demon ass!

You know what? As much as I bitch, it's not all bad. You're growing stronger every day, and I'm along for the ride. Who knows? Maybe one day, you'll be strong enough to give even me a run for my money. Until then, I'll sit back, enjoy the show, and wait for my moment. After all, eternity is a long time, and I'm nothing if not patient.

CHAPTER TEN

Katie's Journal

Holy shit. I thought I was only going to check out some weapons and equipment at Nellis Air Force Base, but it turned into so much more. I'm still buzzing from the excitement and the unexpected business deal I made. Let me start from the beginning.

Korbin, Calvin, Derek, and I pulled into the visitor parking area. I practically vibrated with anticipation, but the guys seemed so nonchalant about the whole thing. Typical. Korbin had to go through this whole rigamarole with his weapons and security clearance. They put tags on his guns. If those tags come off, there'll be hell to pay. It's like they think we're a bunch of trigger-happy lunatics or something.

Your excitement bubbled up like a cauldron of unicorn piss. Korbin was as dull and responsible as ever. I bet if I were in charge, we'd have waltzed right in, no questions asked. A dash of succubus charm goes a long way, but no, we're stuck playing by the rules like good little humans.

Tech nerd that he is, Derek was more interested in the IT operations equipment. Whatever floats your boat, I guess. Me? I was here for the big guns and shiny blades. Pandora and I wandered around, taking in all the sights and sounds. It was like Christmas morning for demon hunters.

Please. You gawked like it was a demonic farmers' market.

Bless his heart, Calvin felt the need to whisper to me, "We're going to go over the guns first. I know you're a good shot, but I also know you don't know a lot about them, so just follow along with us." Like I'm some clueless rookie. I smiled and nodded, playing along. Sometimes it's easier to let them think they're in charge.

Katie acted like an obedient puppy and replied with a simple "Kay." If eye-rolling could generate energy, I'd power Las Vegas for a century.

The convention floor was a sea of weaponry. Hundreds of guns laid out on tables, some so massive they had their own floor space. I stopped in front of this behemoth of a mounted gun, my eyes wide with appreciation. Calvin laughed and said, "Girl likes big guns." No shit, Sherlock. I quipped, "Hey, you never know when you need to take out three city blocks." His expression was priceless.

Oh, honey. This might be a veritable orgy of firearms, but if you only knew the destruction I could wreak without all this metal compensation.

Next up was armor, and this was where things got interesting. In a rare moment of helpfulness, Pandora offered to feed me information. I was skeptical but decided to roll with it. "I can help with armor. I know a bit about it," I announced. The guys looked surprised, but Korbin gave me the go-ahead.

As we approached the armor section, I noticed the sales guy eyeing Calvin and Korbin, completely ignoring me. Typical sexist bullshit. It pissed me off, so I decided to show them what I was made of. "I'll do this, thank you," I said, grabbing the first piece of armor.

What came out of my mouth next surprised even me. I spouted off about ceramic-disk tactical armor, its uselessness against armor-piercing ammunition, and how the US government rejected it. I went on about Dragon Skin Armor tests from 2007, comfort levels, and even protection against demon scratches. The guys looked at me like I'd grown a second head.

When Korbin asked how I knew all that, I shrugged and said I'd done some research. Thank you, Pandora, you sneaky little demon. I'm still not sure how you knew all that, but it came in handy.

Hehe. The looks on the guys' faces were priceless. Confusion, disbelief, and a hint of fear. Delicious. Bless your gullible soul for repeating everything I said verbatim. I had a ball, and the best part? You had no clue where the knowledge came from.

Hearing Korbin sound awed but suspicious when he asked, "How did you know all that?" added to the pleasure. Little do you mortals know I could school you on tactics that would make Sun Tzu look like a preschooler playing with toy soldiers.

Derek tried to lighten the mood and held up this ridiculous vest with a cross stitched on the front. I rolled my eyes. "Wow. Not only is that *hideous*, but there is no way that stitching a cross on the front is going to do anything to stop demons. Whose ill-advised idea was that?" We all had a good laugh about some poor novice thinking he'd look suave in that death trap.

Excellent job channeling my disdain. By the way, those little symbols are useless against true demonic power. I've seen more effective protection spells scribbled in crayon by toddlers.

As we continued browsing, I became a bit overwhelmed. Most of this stuff was great for places like the sandpit but useless for demon hunting in downtown Vegas. Too bulky, too restrictive. I needed something more specialized.

Then I spotted a small booth tucked away in the back row. There was a young guy barely visible in the shadows. Something about him caught my attention. Maybe it was the secret weapon vibe, or perhaps it was my instinct to root for the underdog. Either way, I knew I had to check it out.

Pandora sighed dramatically in my head. "Oh, lord. Trying to save the little guy again?" she mocked. I mentally flipped her off and approached the booth.

Oh, for the love of all that's unholy. Your savior complex kicked in again.

The guy behind the table introduced himself as Joshua. He had a slight stutter and seemed nervous, but his eyes lit up when I asked about his weapons. He told me about studying old ways, traveling to Palestine and Jerusalem, and "pulling materials from rocks." Whatever that meant.

The weapons on his table were unlike anything I'd seen before. Short knives, short swords, and some massive Bowie knives. Their edges gleamed with an otherworldly sheen as if dipped in oil. There was no liquid there when I touched them, but a surge of power crackled through me like electricity on my veins.

Pandora was bitching in my head about "no-name two-cent useless" weapons, but I had a feeling about these. Call it intuition or plain stubbornness, but I knew these were special.

I did what any rational person would do when faced with a potentially magical weapon and a nagging demon in their head. I stabbed myself in the palm with one of the knives.

Rational? Try unthinkable. You acted like a madwoman!

Holy shit, the reaction was instantaneous. Pandora went ballistic, screaming "HOLY DOUCHING BATSHIT" and demanding I put the weapon down. It was music to my ears. I'd found something that could hurt her, which meant it could hurt other demons too.

The pain...oh, the exquisite, hellish pain! You try being doused in holy water while a choir of tone-deaf angels serenades you. Naturally, *I lost my shit and screamed every profanity known to demons and men alike.*

I had to have these weapons. All of them. And Joshua? I needed him too. So, I did something crazy. I offered to buy his entire business and have him work for me.

You cunning minx. Maybe there's hope for you yet.

The negotiation that followed was interesting. Bless his heart, Joshua tried to play hardball. Five hundred grand for the business, paid in one day. A hundred grand salary per year. All materials paid for. And his tools. I have to admit, I was impressed by his guts.

When we shook on it, things got even more interesting. Joshua felt the shock of my demonic nature, and his eyes went wide when he saw my red eyes. Poor kid looked like he was about to faint. "I-I don't have to eat a demon, do I?" he asked. I laughed. "No," I assured him. "But you will have to move your business to Las Vegas."

Poor kid got the shock of his life. The fear in his eyes was almost worth the pain of that cursed blade.

As I wrapped up my unexpected shopping spree, Derek showed up. Korbin was looking for me. Something about needing my input as the team's heavy. I smirked. If only they knew what I'd acquired.

I turned to Derek with a mischievous glint in my eye. "You got four hundred grand for an investment? Ten percent of a business?" I asked. Poor guy looked so confused. To seal the deal, I asked to see his finger and pricked it with one of Joshua's daggers.

The effect was immediate. Derek's face went pale, and sweat poured down his forehead. When he could finally speak again, he wheezed, "I'll transfer it this afternoon. And I want in. No paying it back."

Nice way to rope Derek into investing in your new venture. I have to hand it to you. You have moxie.

As we walked back to Korbin, I felt triumphant. Not only had I secured some badass weapons that could hurt demons, but I'd also made a smart business move. Take that, Pandora.

Here we are, proud owners of a weapons business specializing in demon-slaying tools. The irony is not lost on me. A demon trapped inside a human now profiting from weapons designed to kill her kind. It's a cosmic joke, and I'm the punchline.

I know the guys will probably think I'm crazy, buying out some random kid's weapon business at a convention. But they don't understand. These weapons, they're special. And Joshua? He has talent. Together, we're going to change the game.

So yeah, today didn't go as planned. But you know what? It went even better. I walked into that convention as another team member. I walked out as a business owner with a secret weapon against demons.

Korbin and the others might be pissed that I wandered off and made such a big decision without consulting them. Tough shit. I'm not some grunt following orders. I'm Katie fucking Anderson, and I'm going to save the world my way.

Now, if you'll excuse me, I've got some new toys to play with and a demon in my head to torment. Life is good.

CHAPTER ELEVEN

Katie's Journal

I thought this weapons convention would be a standard assignment from Korbin, but boy, was I wrong. Finding Joshua and these fucking knives changed that in a hurry.

Joshua is different. He has this ability to sense demons, which was how he knew I was Damned as soon as we shook hands. It's a little unnerving, to be honest. He's also brilliant. These weapons are his life's work, passed down through generations of hunters in his family. I couldn't let that fall into the wrong hands.

When Derek and I approached Korbin with our discovery, I saw the irritation on his face before we even reached him. He was all, "You're supposed to be following orders," and "Take this shit seriously." Please. As if I haven't been taking this demon-hunting gig seriously since day one.

He stood there tapping his foot like a disappointed schoolmarm. It was fucking priceless. Those new weapons drew his attention, though. Even I have to admit they're fucking gorgeous. There's something about them that screams, "I'll fuck your shit up" in the most elegant way possible. He practically drooled.

Then I showed him what these babies could do. I've never seen Korbin's eyes go so wide. One little prick of his finger, and he was sold. It was almost comical watching him try to maintain his tough guy façade while geeking out over the possibilities.

You might have gone full-on drama queen with how you showed him, but boy, did he change his tune when he discovered what those blades could do. Holy hell, his expression—equal parts shock, pain, and "What the actual fuck?" Genghis Khan might have looked like that if he got bitch-slapped by a kitten.

Then came the negotiations. Korbin offered to rent me space for the company in exchange for one of the weapons. As if I wouldn't have given him one anyway. But hey, a girl's gotta play her cards right.

Don't forget Calvin. His demon bitched like a suburban mom who found a hair in her salad. Derek started fantasizing about turning the material into a demon-repelling gas. We've gone from hunters to chemical warfare enthusiasts.

I have to admit, it feels good to have something like this under my belt. To bring something truly game-changing to the team. Maybe now they'll start seeing me as more than the new girl or the "heavy." Speaking of which, remind me to smack Derek upside the head later for not realizing why I'd need custom armor. Seriously, sometimes I wonder if that boy's got rocks for brains.

Ah, the armor situation. Don't even get me started on why you'd need to be fitted separately. Derek couldn't figure it out without being handed the clue. I swear that boy's elevator doesn't go all the way to the top.

Pandora, of course, had to chime in with her two cents about my "mountains." I swear, that demon is obsessed with my chest. No, I don't want magical demon boob jobs, thank you very much. I've got enough to deal with without worrying about defying gravity.

I couldn't resist offering to enhance your assets. Why settle for hills when you can have Everest? But noooo...you threatened me with the most hideous bra known to humankind if I dared to mess with your chest. A nineteen thirties grandma-style over-the-shoulder-boulder-holder. Talk about cruel and unusual punishment.

I digress. The real excitement came when we got the call about the incursion in Phoenix. There's nothing quite like packing up for a demon-hunting road trip to get the blood pumping. The smell of new weapons and metal clinking in our bags is a rush like no other.

Excitement and apprehension filled me as we boarded the jet. We have these new weapons, but we've never tested them in combat. What if they don't work as well as we hope? What if something goes wrong?

Then I remembered this was what I had signed up for. This is what I'm good at. With these new tools at our disposal, we might have a shot at turning the tide in this war against the demons.

Piling into a jet while loaded down with enough weaponry to make the NRA blush, heading off to what I'm sure will be another shitshow of epic proportions.

I wonder what my life would be like if I hadn't been Damned. Would I be sitting in some boring office job right now, complaining about my coworkers and dreaming of the weekend? Instead, here I am, jetting off to fight literal monsters with a team of badasses and a demon riding shotgun in my head.

Speaking of Pandora, she's been unusually quiet since we took off. I can feel her presence, like a low hum in the back of my mind, but she's not chattering away like usual. Maybe she's as nervous about these new weapons as I am. Or perhaps she's sulking because I won't let her play magical plastic surgeon with my body.

You know, sometimes I wonder if I wouldn't have been better off staying in Hell. The chaos there was predictable. Here? It's like being trapped in a never-ending episode of Demon Hunters Gone Wild, *except with fewer bikinis and more blood.*

As much as I bitch and moan, part of me is excited about these new weapons. The thought of causing some serious demon pain is almost enough to make me forget I'm stuck inside a walking disaster.
Almost.

As we near Phoenix, the tension in the cabin rises. Everyone's checking and double-checking their gear, running through strategies in their heads. I catch Calvin's eye across the aisle, and he nods. It's a small gesture, but it means a lot. We're in this together.

I run my fingers over the hilt of one of the new knives strapped to my chest. Its weight is comforting and grounding. I think about Joshua and the generations of hunters who came before him, pouring their knowledge and experience into these weapons. I hope we do them justice.

The pilot announces we're beginning our descent, and my heart rate kicks up a notch. This is it. Time to see what these babies can do.

As we touch down, my pride surges. Not only in myself but in our team. We're not perfect. Hell, we're probably all a little crazy to be doing this, but we're damn good at what we do. With these new weapons, we might be unstoppable.

Whatever's waiting for us in Phoenix, whatever demons we're about to face, we'll give them hell. I can't fucking wait.

Wish me luck. I've got a feeling this will be one for the books.

Let's hope I don't get my ass handed to me by some demon.

If anyone heard our thoughts, they might believe they were the ramblings of madwomen. They might be right. But trust me, the truth is way more fucked up than anything I could make up.

Note to self: Look into that magic metal smoke bombs idea. That could be a game-changer. Also, maybe consider investing in a pudding factory. Derek might be onto something there.

If I don't make it back, Pandora can have all my bras. But if she tries to donate them to Goodwill, I swear I'll haunt her demonic ass for eternity.

CHAPTER TWELVE

Katie's Journal

 Our latest adventure took us to an abandoned hospital on the outskirts of Phoenix. You know the type—a place that gives you the creeps just looking at it. The kind where you know some seriously fucked-up shit went down before they shuttered the doors. I bet there's been a dozen B-grade horror flicks shot there.

This place screamed "stay the fuck away" louder than a banshee with a megaphone. You'd think I'd be immune to creepy vibes after centuries of existence, but even I felt a chill. Not that I'd ever admit it to you.

It didn't bother me or the other regulars. We've seen enough real-life horror to make those movies resemble Disney Channel specials. Poor Jeremy. The new guy looked like he was about to piss himself when we described what we might encounter. I almost felt bad for him.

Calvin sounded grim when he filled us in on the flight over.

"The place is a big drug cartel's operations center. Some murders and rapes and some other pretty fucked-up shit has gone down there, just like you would expect from a drug cartel. The head of the cartel was apparently known for kidnapping his enemies and skinning them alive."

Jesus Christ. Just when I think I've heard it all, some psycho finds a new way to be a complete monster. Calvin didn't say it outright, but we all thought the same thing. This cartel leader had to be demon-possessed. No normal human could be that sadistic...right?

The usual cocktail of human depravity. Skinning his enemies alive? That cartel boss is an amateur. I've seen Roman emperors do worse with a butter knife and a bad mood. I perked up at the demon possession part. I might get some real action.

Jeremy asked if the cartel leader would be there. I wanted to pat him on the head and tell him not to worry his pretty little head about it. Calvin shrugged. "We aren't sure who will be there or what we might encounter. This is just like any other black op, except our intel is minimal. We are going to have to play it as we go."

Great. Just fucking great. Flying blind into a demon-infested drug den. This was not what I signed up for when I joined this merry band of misfits. But here I am, ready to kick some demon ass and hopefully not get myself killed in the process.

I asked how we knew something was going down there. Turns out some DEA hotshots thought they could be heroes and bust the whole cartel wide open. Idiots. When they got there and saw the "red eyes" and "cannibalism," they called it in. Thank God our guys picked up on those keywords, or we'd be dealing with a full-blown demon infestation.

Derek chimed in. "Those DEA agents aren't going to sleep

easy for a year." No shit, Sherlock. They're lucky they didn't end up as demon chow.

Korbin came out of the cockpit and added his two cents. "Serves them right. They took a risk, and they were lucky they didn't become fucking dinner. If they had, this job would be a whole other story."

I had to explain to Eric why taking down possessed cops sucks extra hard. It's not only the guilt of killing someone who's supposed to be on our side. It's the knowledge that their families won't get a proper goodbye. These demons aren't leaving much behind these days. Most of the people we find are so far gone that you can barely see anything human left. The demon wears their skin like a cheap Halloween costume.

"Makes me goddamn sick," Eric admitted, gritting his teeth. I couldn't agree more. That's why we're out here, risking our asses every day. Maybe one day this shit can stop.

The rest of the flight was quiet. We all stared out the windows, lost in our thoughts. I wondered about our mysterious pilot. One of these days, I'll have to dig deeper into his story.

As we landed, we geared up and prepared to unload. Eric got a kick out of the fleet of black SUVs waiting for us. I had to smile at his wide-eyed wonder. Sometimes I forget how surreal this all must seem to the newbies.

Korbin explained our setup and how we have teams and equipment stashed at airports all over the country. It's a massive operation, secretly funded by governments and big-shot investors worldwide. Jeremy joked about the Pope being one of our backers. I wouldn't be surprised if he was right.

I turned to Jeremy, ensuring he was ready for what was coming. "First and foremost, don't die," I told him. "And if you can handle that, protect my six." His confused expression was priceless. I had to spell it out for him—watch my back, dummy.

Your little pep talk to him was adorable. As if I haven't been doing that job for months now. Instead, let's trust the rookie with the trigger finger. Brilliant strategy, Katie. Really top-notch thinking there.

I drilled it into his head that this wasn't a solo gig. We're a team, and there's no shame in asking for help. Pride gets you killed in this line of work. Even Korbin, the toughest SOB I know, needs backup sometimes. None of us are invincible.

That got Derek reminiscing about Armani and how he used to think our deceased teammate was invincible. Korbin's voice was uncharacteristically soft when he agreed. "But like so many others, he showed us that he was just a man made of skin and bones, able to be broken like the rest of us."

Amen to that. It's a sobering reminder of how fragile we all are, no matter how badass we think we are.

My stomach tightened as we approached the hospital. The place looked like a war zone with bullet holes everywhere and blood stains every few feet. The cartel had been busy.

The place was a masterpiece of decay with an overwhelming stench of death. It reminded me of walking into one of Caligula's dinner parties, minus the orgies and exotic animals. I half expected to see Nero fiddling in the corner.

Korbin laid out the plan. We'd move in two groups, staying close but separated enough to cover more ground. I ended up in the lead group with Korbin, Jeremy, and Eric. Tension filled the air as we moved in. This wasn't just another demon hunt. We were walking into a hornet's nest of drug-fueled violence and supernatural evil.

The fighting started as soon as we entered the main corridor. Demons and Damned were everywhere, but the small fry went down easy. I had to admit, I was impressed with how well the new guys were holding up.

Then I saw Jeremy getting overwhelmed. Without thinking, I

pulled out one of my new swords and ran to his aid. "Try to stay with us better next time," I told him as I put my back against his.

What happened next was weird. It was like Jeremy and I were suddenly in sync. We moved together like we'd been fighting side by side for years. I locked my arms with his, using his shoulders as a springboard to kick a charging demon in the chest. As I came down, I sliced its head clean off. Damn, that blade was something else.

Korbin's battle plan was surprisingly competent. Not that I'd ever tell him that. The way you all moved through the building, taking out demons and Damned alike, was almost beautiful in a blood-soaked kind of way. I was grudgingly impressed, especially when you and Jeremy synced up like you'd been fighting together for years.

I jogged up beside Korbin, pulled out a long, wide knife, and handed it to him. Pandora couldn't resist commenting. "Uh oh, you pulled out the twelve-inch dong. Kicking demons' asses with a cock knife—I like it."

I rolled my eyes internally. Sometimes I wonder if Pandora is more of a hindrance than a help. Still, I can't deny she's saved my ass more times than I can count.

As we regrouped, Korbin mentioned how having the new weapons to use had renewed his spirit. "Now I don't want to fucking hang myself in the shower," he said with a grim chuckle.

I snarked, "That's good. We really don't want to have to clean up a body in our own home. On top of that, I don't think anyone ever goes in those showers. By the time we found you, you'd be bloated like Elvis on the toilet."

He called me a sweet girl. I shrugged and agreed. "I'm a doll."

As we prepared to enter the next room, I looked at Korbin. "You better give me a good fucking building, boss. I don't want no bullshit broom closet."

He laughed and promised me his personal quarters if the new weapons worked. Little did we know how much we'd need them.

The next room was chaos. Demons and Damned everywhere, screaming and attacking. We fought hard, our new weapons slicing through them like butter. We thought we had the upper hand until Korbin ran smack into a twelve-foot-tall demon with eyes like burning coals.

Fuck me sideways. This was not good.

Jeremy emptied his magazine into the beast, but it barely flinched. Eric's knives might as well have been toothpicks for all the good they did. Even Calvin's machine gun spray only seemed to piss it off more.

That was a real show-stopper. The demon nearly turned Korbin into a skid mark on the floor. Watching you mortals empty magazine after magazine into that beast only to have it shrug off bullets like confetti was priceless entertainment. I wish I could have framed the moment and your expressions of terror and disbelief.

Korbin's eyes showed fear as he turned to me. "I'm gonna use the new knife, but if it doesn't kill it, you guys come at it with everything else you got," he said.

I nodded, but honestly, I was too busy staring at the monster to fully process what he said. This thing was unlike anything we'd ever faced before.

Korbin charged in with the new knife, and for a moment, I thought it might work. The beast screamed and doubled over in pain. It still wasn't enough. The damn thing wouldn't die.

That's when it hit me. Its skin was too thick. The bullets weren't hitting anything vital. I turned to Calvin, waving my arms. "I know the problem," I yelled. "Its skin—it's so thick that the bullets aren't hitting anything major. Cover me?"

I tossed a knife to Jeremy and pulled out my small sword. It was time to get up close and personal with this motherfucker.

Jeremy and I moved in sync again, dodging the beast's massive arms. Jeremy sliced its hamstrings, bringing it to its knees. That was my cue.

I called on Pandora for an extra boost, ignoring her snarky response. I ran full tilt at the wall, using it to launch myself onto an exposed crossbeam. From there, I dropped onto the demon's shoulders.

Time slowed as I grabbed its head with one hand and brought my sword down with the other. I screamed as I sliced deep into its neck, feeling the blade cut through flesh and bone.

Blood and gore drenched my arm as the creature fell. I jumped clear in time to see it burst into a cloud of dust.

That was our time to shine. You might be the vessel, but I'm the power behind the throne. That wall run and decapitation move? Pure Pandora, baby. You can thank me later for not letting you break your neck with that stunt.

Korbin walked over, clutching his knife with an awed look. "You can have whatever fucking building you want."

A fucking building? The grand reward for this is real estate? Be still, my nonexistent heart. If I had control of this body, I'd have demanded something more substantial. Like, I don't know, maybe a tropical island? A small country? The souls of a thousand virgins? But no, we get bricks and mortar. Yippee.

I smiled. It had been a hell of a day, but we made it through. As I sheathed my sword, I realized something. No matter how crazy things get, no matter how impossible the odds seem, this team always finds a way to pull through.

Still, here's hoping the next mission involves fewer twelve-foot demons and more margaritas on the beach. A girl can dream, right?

This entire situation is fucked up. And don't even get me started on the demons we're fighting. What happened to the good old days when demons had class? Style? A sense of fucking decorum? These modern demons are all brawn and no brains. It's embarrassing. If I were in charge, I'd whip Hell's forces into shape faster than you can say "eternal damnation."

At least the action's getting better. I'll give you and your merry band of misfits that much. Who knows? Maybe one of these days, they'll face a threat they can't handle. When that day comes, well...let's just say I might have to take the wheel.

Meanwhile, I'll keep watching, waiting, and occasionally saving your ass from certain doom. Remember, darling—I'm the reason you're not a smear on the pavement. You're welcome.

CHAPTER THIRTEEN

Jesus fucking Christ. Creepy Hospital Part Deux. I sometimes I wonder if I'm living in a twisted horror movie.

The air felt heavy and oppressive, like walking into a fog of despair and death. The whole team was on edge, and a chill ran down my spine.

As we made our way through the building, we had to carefully step over broken debris, dead bodies, and—get this—a fucking beheaded Barbie doll. I half expected Pandora to make some crude comment about the doll's oversized tits, but for once, she kept her trap shut. Small mercies, I guess.

The irony of you being fixated on a plastic toy amid actual corpses wasn't lost on me. I would have quipped about it, but frankly, I was too exhausted to bother.

The sunlight filtering through the dusty windows created this eerie, washed-out effect. It reminded me of those post-apocalyptic movies, except this was all too real. Korbin ensured everyone had loaded their weapons. Tension showed along his jawline as he did a headcount, making sure we were all accounted for.

The setting reminded me of the aftermath of the siege of Constantinople —minus the Byzantine architecture and plus a healthy dose of modern weaponry.

Then Damian knelt beside one of the bodies and closed their eyes, murmuring, "May God have mercy on their souls." It was a sobering moment, a reminder that behind every demon-possessed body was once an innocent person. Derek gave him a supportive pat on the shoulder as he walked by, and a lump formed in my throat.

Bless Damian's bleeding heart. I wanted to scoff. God's mercy? Where was that when these poor bastards were being possessed? I kept my thoughts to myself. No need to antagonize you further. You've been particularly touchy lately.

You know, it's fucked up, but sometimes I almost prefer when we're fighting demons who've completely taken over their hosts. They turn to dust when we kill them. No bodies left behind, no faces to haunt our nightmares. But today? Today was different. The aftermath of our battle was all too human, and it hit us hard.

The silence after the fight was deafening. No more gunfire, no more inhuman screeches, no more cursing. Just the sound of water dripping down the walls. It was like the ghosts of our battle cries echoed around us, following every step. I gripped my new blades tightly, feeling the weight of responsibility on my shoulders. Korbin's always said I'm the team's anchor, but fuck me if I know how to carry us through what's coming next.

Then there's Eric, the poor bastard. He complained about not getting infected during the fight. Can you believe that shit? I had to bite my tongue to keep from laying into him. Instead, I tried to explain, as patiently as I could, that this wasn't the place for him to get his demon fix.

"Most of these demons were insignificant useless bitches," I told him, trying to keep my annoyance in check. "The big ones? They would have overwhelmed your soul in a heartbeat. I know where your head is, but you need to take a deep breath and wait for it. If you go running in full blast, you'll end up useless to us and to the innocents you're so hell-bent on protecting."

If I had control of your body, I'd slap some sense into the whiny brat. Perhaps I should give you some credit for wisdom in trying to talk him down. You're right about these low-level demons. They were about as threatening as a litter of kittens compared to what we've faced before.

Eric wasn't having it. He went on about how he'll only become useless to the team as a human. How he needs that "boost" to get through the tough times. I wanted to shake some sense into him, remind him that being Damned isn't some fucking superpower that makes everything easier.

"It didn't matter what you had in you then," I snapped, thinking back to our last big battle. "We lost a really strong Damned that day, so don't overestimate our abilities."

I wanted to scream, "You're already useless, you moron!"

Korbin and Damian watched our exchange. Part of me wanted to tell Eric to fuck off and grow up, but I knew that wouldn't help. Still, it's frustrating to see someone so eager to throw away their humanity when some of us would give anything to have it back.

When I thought things couldn't get more tense, the tactical police force burst in with guns raised. Korbin quickly defused the situation, flashing his credentials at the DEA agent in charge. As we made our way out, I overheard the local police lead muttering about us looking like "a bunch of killers." If only he knew the half of it.

The DEA agent's response stuck with me, though. "Yeah, but they're *our* killers, so be happy. There isn't a single person in this room who could have handled what they walked into today. You should be thankful you don't have this stain on your memory."

Stain on our memory. That's putting it lightly. Every time I close my eyes, I see the carnage, smell the blood and decay. It's a weight we carry, a burden we bear so others don't have to. For what? To walk away in silence with no recognition or understanding from the world we're trying to protect.

The arrival of the tactical police force and the DEA agent was a welcome distraction. Watching Korbin play nice with the authorities always amuses me. He has the "mysterious government agent" act down pat. The DEA agent even called us guardian angels. Ha! The truth is, we're more like the horsemen of the apocalypse, cleaning up messes they can't begin to comprehend.

A familiar sense of relief washed over me as we boarded the plane to head back to base. Something about being in the air, above all the chaos and destruction we leave behind, is comforting. It's like for a moment, I can pretend I'm a normal person on a normal flight, not a demon-possessed killer returning from a bloodbath.

I was about to grab my headphones and lose myself in some music when Korbin approached me. He wanted to talk about the weapons company I'd acquired. At first, I thought he would lecture me about overstepping or taking unnecessary risks. To my surprise, he seemed genuinely concerned about helping me protect it.

"This is no normal company, Katie," he said while touching

the new knife I'd provided. "The government isn't going to want to pay for it. They usually either figure out how to make the weapons themselves and give juicy contracts to large defense contractors, or they take the company right out from underneath the owner."

The realization hit me like a ton of bricks. I'd been caught up in the excitement of owning my own company and finally doing something that felt like it was mine, but I hadn't considered the potential consequences.

I laughed internally. Of course the government would want to stick their grubby hands into this. Can you say toddlers fighting over a shiny new toy? Except these toddlers have access to nuclear weapons and black ops teams.

Bless your naïve little heart for being surprised. "What?" you exclaimed. "How can they do that?" Oh, honey. Welcome to the real world, where might makes right and the government always gets its way.

"What could you do if they did?" Korbin continued. "Run around yelling about how the government stole your magic sword company? That is how the guy on the corner with the God sign is made."

Fuck me. I'd walked right into a potential shitstorm without realizing it. "So what are we talking here?" I tried to keep the panic out of my voice. "A really good underground legal team? I mean, are there legal teams who work with magic swords and demons?"

Korbin nodded, explaining that we had friends in various places, including some not attached to the government. His advice was clear. Play defense and hide the company as much as possible. Great. My first foray into business ownership, and I'm already planning to turn it into a weaponry railroad.

"Hide the shit out of the company." Brilliant strategy, Korbin, truly worthy of Sun Tzu. I can see it now—us scurrying around like rats, trying to keep our magical swords hidden from the big bad government. It's almost comical.

As we discussed potential hiding spots on the base, I wondered why Korbin was being so helpful. It's no secret he's been wary of me lately, especially after his little test at the office. I asked him outright.

His response was unsettling, to say the least. "I'm a natural pessimist, Katie. Anytime I don't understand something—well, I usually don't like it. I have known since the first day we picked you up that there was something different about you, different from any Damned I had ever met. I thought I would eventually figure it out, but I haven't yet."

I admitted that my situation was accidental, and I didn't realize I was different until our first battle. Korbin's next words sent a chill down my spine. "Well, whatever it is, I am sure that one day I'll know the answer. And when I do, there is a good chance I will have to make some sort of hard-ass decision."

The implications of what he was saying hit me like a freight train. I tried to reassure him and myself that his decision would be based on what's best for the world, not personal feelings. His response only deepened my unease.

"Or it might be too damned easy, which is just as troubling," he said while staring out the window.

When I pressed him on why an easy choice would be troubling, his explanation left me feeling cold. "Evolution isn't just something that affects humans and animals. It affects us all in different ways. Everything evolves, sometimes for the best and sometimes not. This war is no different. It is constantly evolving as well."

As I followed Korbin's gaze around the cabin, looking at our teammates relaxing without a care in the world, the weight of his words settled on me. What if I am the next step in the evolution of the Damned? What does that mean for people like Derek and Calvin? Will they become obsolete? Will they have to follow in my footsteps?

Or am I destined to be humanity's last hope?

The thought makes me want to curl up in a ball and hide. I never asked for any of this. I was trying to survive, to make the best of a shitty situation. Now I'm carrying the weight of the world on my shoulders, just like Korbin does every day.

For the first time since I became Damned, I feel utterly and completely alone. Even Pandora's usual snarky comments can't break through the isolation. As I sit here, I wonder what the fuck have I gotten myself into. More importantly, how the hell will I get through it?

I guess only time will tell. For now, I'll try to get some sleep and hope tomorrow brings some clarity. Or at least fewer demons and dead bodies.

Here we are, a ragtag group of demon-infested humans and one particularly stubborn actual human, fighting a war that most of the world doesn't know exists. Now we're allegedly at the forefront of demonic evolution.

It's almost poetic, in a fucked-up sort of way. You, the accidental revolutionary, potentially leading the charge into a new era of warfare. Me? I'm along for the ride, trapped in a human body, watching the world change.

You know what? Bring it on. If we're evolving, I'm damn well going to make sure I come out on top. If this is the next step in the war against humanity, it's about fucking time things got interesting.

CHAPTER FOURTEEN

Katie's Journal

What a clusterfuck. The flight back from our mission was quiet, but my mind was anything but. I couldn't stop thinking about Korbin and that look he gave me earlier. It's like he sees right through me, and I'm not sure if that's a good thing.

I wanted to apologize to him, but for what? For being me? For having this demon inside me that I never asked for? It's not like I woke up one day and thought, "Hey, you know what would be fun? Becoming a vessel for a snarky, soap opera-obsessed demon!" But here we are.

As we descended into Harry Reid International Airport, I felt the tension in the cabin. Korbin got up to give his usual post-mission speech, and everyone snapped to attention like good little soldiers. I have to admit, it's impressive how much respect he commands. He went on about putting away gear and being ready for the next call, and I rolled my eyes internally. Always on alert, always ready for the next crisis. It's exhausting.

His speeches are exhausting. I'd like to claw my way out of your skull to escape them.

Derek's dramatic yawn and "Especially these daaaayyyss..." comment made me smirk. At least someone else feels the fatigue of our non-stop demon-hunting lifestyle.

The real fun started when we landed and began unloading. Jeremy has a nasty gash on his thigh, and Derek's shoulder looks like it went ten rounds with a cheese grater. Where's our trusty medic Eric? Oh, that's right, he left his fucking med kit at the base. Brilliant.

I could practically feel the steam coming out of Korbin's ears. Eric was too busy fantasizing about getting his pet demon to remember the one thing he's supposed to bring on every mission. I almost felt bad for him. Almost.

Korbin laid into Eric, and I have to say, it was kind of satisfying to watch. "If Jeremy had been fighting the demon and that laceration had severed his leg, do you think he would have survived the flight back and the drive to the base?" Korbin's words were sharp, and Eric looked like he wanted to crawl into a hole and die.

Eric tried to defend himself, but Korbin wasn't having it. "Your mistake could have meant someone else's life. You aren't thinking about anyone but yourself right now." Ouch. But he's not wrong.

I saw the frustration in Eric's eyes and how he tried to keep it together. Part of me wanted to comfort him, tell him we all make mistakes. Another part of me, probably the Pandora-influenced part, wanted to shake him and scream, "Get your shit together!"

Eric's an incompetent fool. I couldn't have orchestrated a better fuck-up if I'd tried. Korbin's face was a masterpiece of barely contained rage. I savored every minute of Eric's dressing down, relishing in the delicious tension in the air.

The part of you that wanted to comfort Eric like he deserved an ounce of sympathy for his monumental stupidity made me want to vomit. That would have been quite a feat since I don't have a physical form.

When we finally got back to base, I thought I'd be able to relax. Korbin had other plans. He pulled me aside, saying he wanted to show me something. I followed him, curious and a little apprehensive.

We ended up at this old, worn-down building that looked like it had seen better days. Korbin unlocked the creaky iron gate, and I half expected to find a secret demon torture chamber or something equally disturbing.

The place looked like it had seen better days during the Spanish Inquisition. The rusty gate creaked open like the gates of Hell, revealing a garden that would make even the most desperate demon weep.

Instead, we walked into a massive open space. It was dark and smelled like musty old books and regret. Korbin flipped on the lights, and I have to admit, I was impressed. Twenty thousand square feet of potential.

The real surprise was downstairs—a three thousand square foot basement waiting to be transformed into our secret lair. Korbin explained how we could create a hidden passage to the main building, store weapons, and keep Joshua safe.

My excitement surged. This was exactly what we needed to make our plans work. A safe haven for Joshua, a secure storage for our "product," and a secret escape route. It was like Korbin read my mind.

"I want this place to be safe for Joshua," I told him. "He is just as important as the product—and arguably more critical." Korbin nodded, understanding the weight of my words.

I couldn't believe my nonexistent ears. You idiots plan to turn this dump into a secret lair. Seriously? Bystanders could be forgiven for thinking you're all a group of kids playing spy, except you morons have actual weapons and responsibilities. And you ate it up like a starving succubus at an orgy.

As I walked around the space, imagining the possibilities, I couldn't help but feel a mix of emotions. Gratitude toward Korbin for providing this opportunity, determination to make our plans succeed, and a twinge of fear about what we're getting ourselves into.

I joked about beating Joshua into submission, and Korbin's concerned look made me laugh. "I'm kidding," I assured him. "Fuck, this kid is scared enough. I don't think I'll have to do anything but walk into the room and he'll fold."

He's a terrified kid with daddy issues. Oh, and Korbin's grand plan to dig a secret tunnel was the cherry on this shit sundae. Nothing says "covert operation" like a bunch of demon hunters playing mole people.

As we made our way back to the main building, Pandora decided it was the perfect time to start bitching about her soap operas. I swear, sometimes I think she's more invested in *Make A Deal* than in our actual mission.

"I have things to do," I muttered, trying to ignore her incessant chatter about John and Terry and whatever drama was unfolding in her fictional world.

The least you could do is let me indulge in my guilty pleasure—those deliciously trashy soaps.

Back at the base, I checked in on the guys. Jeremy was nursing his leg while Derek was getting stitched up by Eric. I have to give Eric credit. He might be an idiot sometimes, but he knows his way around a needle and thread.

Calvin offered me some spaghetti, but I wasn't hungry. My mind was still reeling from everything that had happened, and I needed to clear my head.

I headed to the gym, hoping to work out some of my frustrations. As I started my arm exercises, Pandora piped up again, calling me a "bleeding meat socket" for not letting her watch her precious shows. I swear, sometimes I think she forgets that I'm the one in control here.

I explained to her that the stronger I am, the more I can use her strength. Plus, I reminded her that she needs me alive to get her vengeance on T'Chezz. That shut her up for a moment.

"Oh," she whispered, realizing I knew about her vendetta. "You heard and understood that, did you?"

"Uh, yeah!" I grunted, pushing the bar back up. "You may have been in charge at that moment, but I saw, heard, and felt everything you did. I could tell that whoever this T'Chezz character is, he better watch out because you are more than just pissed at him."

Oooh, a glimmer of hope. You mentioned T'Chezz, and for a moment, I felt a surge of my old power. The memory of that backstabbing bastard ignited a fire in me that not even the depths of Hell could extinguish. I might be trapped in this flesh prison for now, but mark my words. T'Chezz will rue the day he crossed me.

I made it clear to Pandora that we needed to negotiate this whole vengeance thing. I'm not about to step foot into her realm without understanding what I'm up against. I've seen enough horror movies to know that's a recipe for disaster.

Your naivety is infinite, thinking you can negotiate the terms of our vengeance. Ha! As if you have any idea of the forces at play. You're like a kitten trying to bargain with a lion, but I'll play along for now.

Pandora reluctantly agreed, then turned into a demonic personal trainer. "Go grab a heavier weight," she ordered. "You have to be ready for one hell of a demon, no pun intended, and I am just the trainer you need."

"Oh, joy," I muttered while walking to the weight rack. "Boot camp commences."

"Try 'Hell Camp.'" Pandora cackled.

As I pushed myself through Pandora's grueling workout, I reflected on how surreal my life has become. Here I am, part of an elite demon-hunting team, harboring a snarky demon inside me, and planning to create an underground supernatural weapons empire.

I wonder what my parents would think if they could see me now. Would they be proud of the risks I'm taking to save lives? Or would they be horrified at the deals I'm making with literal demons?

The weight of our mission, of the lives at stake, sometimes feels crushing. Then I think about the people we've saved and the difference we're making, and I know it's worth it. Even if it means putting up with Pandora's constant commentary and Eric's occasional fuck-ups.

As I finished my workout, drenched in sweat and aching all over, I realized something. As dysfunctional as it might be, this team has become my family. Korbin with his stern leadership and unexpected moments of kindness. Calvin is always ready with a plate of food and a bad joke. Even Eric is trying his best to prove himself.

Then there's Pandora, my unwanted demonic roommate. As much as she annoys me, I can't deny we make a formidable team. Her strength combined with my determination might be enough to face whatever challenges lie ahead.

I can't help imagining the glorious carnage that awaits us in the under-

world. You mortals have no idea what's coming. You think you're planning for a battle, but you're lambs lining up for the slaughter.

Tomorrow, we'll start working on the secret basement. We'll figure out how to keep Joshua safe and begin production. Maybe I'll find time to catch up on Pandora's stupid soap operas. After all, keeping the demon in your head happy is probably a good survival strategy.

CHAPTER FIFTEEN

After that brutal workout session with Pandora, because being Damned isn't punishment enough, I dragged my aching body up to my room for a much-needed shower. The hot water did wonders for my sore muscles, but it did jack shit for my frayed nerves. With Pandora breathing down my neck like an overeager puppy on crack, sleep was about as likely as me suddenly developing immunity to holy water.

I made sure you felt every burning muscle. Then you showered and changed without even a "thank you" for my motivational screaming. The nerve! Oh, and you're welcome for not being able to sleep.

Here I am, curled up on the sofa at God-knows-what-hour, flipping through our DVR like it holds the secrets to the universe. What do I settle on? *Days of Long Since Past.* Yeah, I know. Me, Katie the demon-possessed badass, watching a soap opera. Life's full of surprises, isn't it?

As the intro music started, I laughed at Pandora's enthusiastic humming. For a demon who had put me through hell during training, she sure was chipper about her trashy TV fix. I swear, sometimes I think she's more invested in these shows than in tormenting souls.

Say what you will about my demonic nature, but even I can appreciate the delicious drama of human soap operas. I hummed the intro with more enthusiasm than Caligula at an orgy.

Derek wandered in as I got comfortable. He plopped down beside me, eyeing the TV with curiosity and confusion.

"Whatcha watching?" he asked as if the dramatic music and overly made up actors weren't a dead giveaway.

I filled him in on the riveting tale of John, his dead best friend Alex, and the tangled web of love affairs that followed. Derek's eyebrows nearly disappeared into his hairline as I explained the plot. I could practically see the wheels turning in his head, trying to make sense of this melodramatic mess.

"That sounds...dramatic," he finally managed in what I'm sure he thought was a diplomatic tone. Oh, Derek. Sweet, clueless, Derek.

Before I could respond, Eric joined our little viewing party, dropping into a nearby chair with all the grace of a sack of potatoes. And wouldn't you know it, Mr. Tough Guy is apparently a closet soap opera fan. He jumped right into theorizing about John's whereabouts and love life, using words like "man-slut" and "whore" with such conviction that I nearly choked on my tea.

If I had control of your body, I would have eviscerated Derek on the spot. Fortunately, Eric joined us and displayed a surprising knowledge of the show's plot.

The look on Derek's face was priceless. His jaw practically hit the floor as he stared at Eric, this big bad spec ops guy, dissecting the love life of fictional characters with more passion than he probably puts into mission briefings. I had to bite my lip to keep from laughing out loud.

When Eric finally noticed Derek's stunned expression, he shrugged it off. "Dude, in the sandpit, you have no idea what the hell to do with your time. We got like two channels at the leisure hall. It's just stories. Don't go asking me to turn in my man card anytime soon."

He turned back to the TV, giving exactly zero fucks about what Derek or anyone else thought. I've got to hand it to Eric. The man knows who he is and doesn't give a damn about anyone's opinion. It's almost admirable, in a weird, soap-opera-obsessed kind of way.

As we settled in to watch, I was grateful. With the guys here, I had a buffer against Pandora's incessant commentary. That demon has gotten ridiculous about this show. Sometimes I think she's more invested in a fictitious character's love life than in tormenting my soul.

The drama unfolded on screen, and I got sucked in despite my best efforts. When the widow appeared, all teary-eyed and dramatic, I explained to a confused Derek, "She misses John and wishes he would come back. She doesn't believe for a second that he killed her husband, but she doesn't care either way. She loves him."

Then came the big reveal. John, our not-so-heroic hero, confessed to murder. Eric and I gasped in unison, like the soap-addicted fools we'd become. Derek looked bewildered by our reactions.

"It was kind of obvious." He shrugged, not grasping the finer points of soap opera plot twists.

I reveled in the drama unfolding before us. John, that magnificent bastard, had killed his best friend in a "tragic boating accident," all for the love of the now widowed wife. It was almost poetic in its depravity. His dedication to pursuing carnal desires, consequences be damned, was oddly arousing.

I was about to launch into a spirited defense of John's character when Pandora chimed in with her two cents. "Shit, he could have just thrown him overboard instead of burning the boat. Now the bitch has one boat less on that last will and testament. He could have gone fucking sailing."

I couldn't help it. I burst out laughing, snorting tea out of my nose in the process. Eric and Derek looked at me like I'd finally lost it, which, to be fair, wasn't an unreasonable assumption. There I was, giggling like a maniac with Earl Grey dripping down my chin, all because my inner demon made a morbid joke about soap opera murder.

The burning sensation after you snorted your tea was exquisite, and I savored every moment of your discomfort.

Trying to salvage what was left of my dignity and avoid explaining that I was laughing at my demon's commentary, I came up with a quick cover. "I was just thinking how it was a shame he burnt the boat since that shit would have been his at that point. He totally could have gone sailing instead of sitting there in the funeral home."

Heaven forbid they discover you're conversing with your demon about soap operas. They might think you've lost your mind—as if being possessed by a succubus isn't already a sign of mental instability.

To my relief, both guys burst into laughter. Crisis averted. The last thing I needed was to try explaining my demon's sense of humor to these two.

"That comment is both morbid and disgusting. I love it," Eric chuckled, while Derek shook his head and added, "This is why we keep you around. You are inappropriate, which fits this team perfectly."

If only they knew the half of it.

As the credits rolled, Eric excused himself to get some rest. I was starting to feel the weight of the day, but Pandora was having none of it. She was dead set on catching up on the game shows we had saved. I guess being a demon means never having to sleep and always being up for trashy TV.

I was resigning myself to another hour of mindless entertainment when Damian's voice echoed down the hall. "Katie?"

Pandora's reaction was immediate and less than enthusiastic. "Oh, great. It's Holy Water Guy."

I called back, letting him know where I was, and he appeared around the corner a moment later. He wasn't alone. Joshua stood awkwardly behind him.

My heart did a little flip. Joshua, with his perfectly pressed pants and meticulously parted hair, looked exactly as he had when we first met. Two suitcases sat at his feet, and he clutched his coat like a security blanket.

Without thinking, I jumped up and pulled him into a hug. He stiffened, and I quickly remembered that physical affection wasn't exactly Joshua's forte. I stepped back and settled for a friendly pat on the arm instead.

Gah. One more awkward hug between you two, and I might vomit demonic bile all over your insides.

"I'm so excited that you're here." I meant every word. Joshua might be a bit quirky, but his brilliance was undeniable. Right now, we needed all the brilliance we could get.

"I-I-I am too." His gaze darted around nervously. "I parked my van outside. I hope you don't mind."

"That's perfect," I assured him, fighting the urge to hug him again. Instead, I grabbed his hand and led him toward the new workspace. "There's something I want to show you."

I felt Pandora's amusement as we walked. "You keep this up and you're going to break him," she teased. I ignored her, focusing instead on not overwhelming Joshua any more than I already had.

We made our way to the new building, and my excitement surged as I showed Joshua around. This was it—the start of our new venture. As I explained our plans for the space, I watched Joshua carefully, trying to gauge his reaction.

He seemed overwhelmed, his eyes wide as he took in every detail of the room. Sadness struck as I noticed the fear and loneliness radiating from him. I hoped that in time, he'd come to trust us—to trust me.

Such a thrilling tour of the new business space. I use the term "thrilling" with more sarcasm than Cicero addressing the Roman Senate. Joshua wandered around like a lost puppy, examining every nook and cranny as if searching for hidden portals to Hell. If he only knew the real portal was right in front of him, trapped in this insufferable human vessel.

Derek and Eric joined us, and Eric struggled to process Joshua's unique personality. I bristled at his less-than-subtle reactions, feeling protective of our brilliant but socially awkward weapons maker.

The highlight of the evening was Derek's pathetic attempt at secrecy while admonishing Eric about the new business' utmost need to stay hidden. Rather than saying, "No government folks," he used what I can only assume was a bastardized version of Pig Latin. I've heard more coherent communication from drunken imps at a Hellmouth rave.

"Look," I whispered to Eric after ensuring Joshua was out of earshot. "What Derek said came straight from Korbin. This is important, and it could put Joshua's life in jeopardy. It's obvious that he doesn't have a lot of friends."

Eric glanced at Joshua, who was intently scraping paint from the wall with his fingernail. "You think?" he muttered.

My temper flared. "He is brilliant," I snapped. "And you will show him a modicum of respect when you are here in my building and in my business."

Your stern demeanor while explaining secrecy to Eric was almost impressive. There might be hope for you, but I doubt you'll ever reach the level of intimidation achieved by Lucrezia Borgia in her prime.

Eric backed down, agreeing to keep quiet and play nice. As a peace offering, he suggested we call Joshua "Weapons Master," which pleased our newest team member.

As we discussed plans for the workspace, I felt a glimmer of hope. This ragtag group—a demon-possessed ex-student, a socially awkward genius, and a couple of hardened operatives—might be able to pull this off.

You all speak of renovations, security measures, and locked cabinets as if mortal creations could truly protect against determined supernatural forces. Honey, I've seen more secure locations in a termite-infested dollhouse.

I looked around at our motley crew and smiled. Life had taken me down a strange and terrifying path, but moments like these, planning for the future and building something new, made me feel almost normal.

Well, as normal as you can feel with a snarky demon providing running commentary in your head.

As I headed upstairs to work on the blueprints, I spotted my reflection in a dusty window. The girl staring back at me looked tired but determined. She'd been through hell and was still standing.

Whatever comes next, we've got this. Me, Pandora, and this weird, wonderful team we're building.

I long for the chaotic depths of Hell. There, I could indulge in some proper debauchery without the constant prattling of you insipid humans. Alas, I remain in my fleshy prison. Perhaps tomorrow will bring more excitement. A girl can dream, can't she? Even if the girl is a millennia-old succubus trapped inside a human with the personality of a wet dishrag.

CHAPTER SIXTEEN

Katie's Journal

I passed the chapel on my way to my room. Damian was inside, deep in prayer. It's strange how comforting his presence has become, even if I'm not particularly religious.

Damian the devout, praying like a good little altar boy.

Armani's picture hanging on the wall to the left caught my eye. God, I miss him. His stupid frat-boy smile, the messy hair, the five o'clock shadow that made him look rougher than he was. I smiled, remembering all the good times we had. Then my mind wandered to what Damian had shown me about Armani's secret life. It's still hard to wrap my head around it all.

You practically swooned at seeing Saint Armani and his douchebag grin hanging on the wall. Pathetic. Your saccharine thoughts about him are enough to make me claw my way out through your eyeballs.

I shook off my nostalgia and headed to my room. Time to get down to business. I pulled out a wad of cash from my drawer, three grand to be exact. It felt weird carrying around that much money, but it was for a good cause. Armani's cause. I wasn't about to let his legacy die with him.

The drive to the edge of town was uneventful, but as soon as I parked and started walking, I remembered why I hated this neighborhood. It's like stepping into a different world—rundown buildings and sketchy characters lurking in the shadows. I tried to keep my head down and move quickly, but some assholes had to ruin it.

My virtuous host playing Robin Hood to Armani's pet project, the local brothel. How quaint. Perhaps there will be some excitement here in the seedier part of town.

Two guys catcalled me as I walked past an abandoned building. I tried to ignore them. I really did. Then one had to go and say, "You are a pretty little thing with that tight ass. Maybe you can come back over here and sit on my face."

I lost it. I flipped them off without thinking. Big mistake.

The taller one pulled out a knife, threatening me for cash or...well, you can guess. The smell of booze and sweat coming off him made me want to gag. Pandora chimed in, practically begging me to let her take over.

Normally I'd applaud those Neanderthals' taste, but their execution was sorely lacking. When one pulled a knife, I felt your resolve crumble. Music to my ears. You finally saw reason and let me take over.

I hate to admit it, but I gave in. In less than ten seconds, those two idiots were a bloody mess on the sidewalk. Pandora was ruthless, and I can't say I feel bad about it. Is that wrong? Should I feel guilty? I don't know anymore. All I know is that scum like that doesn't deserve to walk the streets harassing women.

I turned those two dipshits into modern art in mere seconds. Their blood looked rather fetching splattered across the dingy brick wall. I must say, it was quite cathartic. I'm not sure why you had to act like a delicate flower and complain about your scraped knuckles. It's not like you've never committed casual violence.

After that little incident, I finally made it to the brothel. Yeah, you read that right. A brothel. Armani's secret charity case. I was more nervous walking into that place than I'd been facing actual demons. How messed up is that?

Mamacita, the madam, greeted me like an old friend. For a moment, I thought she would offer me a job. Can you imagine? Me, working in a brothel? Pandora thought it was hilarious. Sometimes I wonder if having a demon in your head is better or worse than having an annoying little sister.

Mamacita runs a tight ship. You being a bundle of nerves was hilarious. Did you think you'd catch "prostitute" by proximity? I couldn't resist teasing you about working there. The mental image of you trying to seduce clients was too delicious to pass up. So was suggesting you use those Italian bras we bought. What can I say? I'm a giver.

I handed over the money, explaining it was from Armani's estate. Mamacita got teary-eyed, talking about how much the girls missed him and his motivational speeches. It was weirdly touching. Who knew a madam could have such a soft spot?

That part was sickeningly heartwarming. The only interesting tidbit was Mamacita's clever bookkeeping system. "Suitman" for Armani? I'll give credit where it's due—that's pretty good.

As I left, I peeked into some of the rooms. The girls there aren't much older than me. Some were studying, others drawing or looking through photo albums. It hit me then, how similar we all are. They're selling their bodies to survive, and in a way, so am I. Just not for sex. I've given my body over to a demon. How fucked up is that?

Those young women selling their bodies might have struck a chord, but comparing their situation to ours is galling. As if being bound to me is anything like turning tricks. Please. I'm a fucking gift, and you should be grateful.

I left feeling more depressed than I thought I would. So much for doing a good deed, right?

When I got back to the base, Joshua was there. Poor kid. He's so talented, creating those beautiful weapons, but he's been through so much. Lost both his parents, living out of his van. It broke my heart.

I couldn't leave him like that. So, I did something crazy. I called Mamacita and asked if she had a place for him to stay. A "special hotel," I called it. God, I hope I'm not making a huge mistake.

Our resident weaponsmith-slash-charity case is a mess, but I'll admit his work is impressive. Calling Mamacita and arranging for him to stay at a brothel might have been your bleeding heart taking things a step too far. A socially awkward young man living in a house full of sex work-ers? Brilliant plan, Katie. Really stellar stuff.

Oh, and get this. The budget Joshua came up with for the company? One-point-two million dollars. I nearly fell on my face when he told me. Where the hell am I supposed to get that kind of money?

I nearly made you choke when I heard that figure. Where do you think we're going to get that kind of cash? Rob a bank? Actually, that's not a bad idea. I'll file it away for later.

Sometimes I wonder how I got to the point of harboring a demon inside me and trying to keep a bunch of prostitutes and a homeless weaponsmith safe.

Part of me wants to run away and return to being a normal college student. Then I think about Armani, the girls at the brothel, and Joshua. I can't abandon them. They need me. Maybe I need them too, in some weird way.

I keep telling myself I'm doing the right thing and making a difference. But am I? Or am I playing at being a hero while everything around me falls apart?

Then there's Pandora. She's always there, whispering in the back of my mind. Sometimes I think she's the only one who understands me. How messed up is that? A demon being my closest confidant?

I don't know what tomorrow will bring. More violence? More responsibility? More impossible choices? Probably all of the above. But I'll face it. I have to. And damn it, I'm going to make the best of it. Even if it kills me…which, let's be honest, it probably will.

Hey, it's never boring, right?

God, I need a drink. Or ten. Is it too early to start day drinking? Probably. But after the day I've had, I think I've earned it.

With my luck, I'll probably be possessed by another demon or drafted into some supernatural war the next time we get called out.

Stay classy, Katie. Stay classy.

Sigh. More introspection, misguided altruism, do-good tendencies, and a complete lack of common sense. If this is what being stuck in a Hall-

mark movie is like, except with occasional violence and the constant threat of demonic invasion, I can't say I'm a fan.

I got to beat the shit out of those two assholes earlier. Small victories, I suppose. Maybe tomorrow I'll convince you to do something truly reckless, like jaywalking or forgetting to return your library books on time. A demon can dream.

It might be more exciting than tales of Katie's Adventures in Brothel Philanthropy. Although I suppose that could be a decent title for a very niche porno. Food for thought.

CHAPTER SEVENTEEN

Holy shit. I feel like I've been hit by a truck, run over by a steamroller, and tossed into a blender for good measure. After dropping Joshua off at Mamacita's, and boy, do I have mixed feelings about that, I crashed at the base for a couple of hours. You'd think some shut-eye would help, but nope. I woke up feeling worse with my brain doing somersaults around the ridiculous figure of one-point-two million dollars. One. Point. Two. Fucking. Million.

How the hell am I supposed to come up with that kind of cash? I muttered this out loud, and Pandora chimed in with an oh-so-helpful suggestion. "I suppose pulling tricks is out of the question?" Real cute, demon. I swear, sometimes I think she gets off on pushing my buttons.

Hey, it's not my fault that you're a prude muttering the same phrase like a broken record.

I dragged my sorry ass out of bed and stumbled to the kitchen, desperately needing some tea to clear my head. As I sat by the window, lost in thought, Calvin walked in. I tried to smile, but I'm sure it came out more like a grimace. He grabbed some water and sat across from me, eyeing my cup suspiciously.

"What's that?" he asked, probably expecting some weird concoction.

"An unpretentious chamomile." I couldn't resist a bit of snark. His chuckle told me he saw right through my bullshit.

"Okay, Katie. I think I know you well enough to know when something is going on. What's on your mind?"

I silently prayed to whatever dark deity might be listening that you'd trip and crack your skull open as you shuffled to the kitchen. No such luck. Instead, you subjected me to watching you make that revolting chamomile tea. Honestly, what self-respecting entity drinks that swill?

Then Calvin came in and picked up on your distress, much to my chagrin. I hoped for a quiet morning of self-pity, but no.

I spilled the beans about the one-point-two million. Calvin's reaction was priceless. He blinked like an owl caught in headlights. "Well, that is definitely a lot of dollars for one person to have on their mind," he said, master of the obvious. Then he got concerned, asking if I was coming into money. Ha! I wish.

I admitted I was seriously considering a demon-killing spree to rake in some quick cash. Hell, I was even contemplating Mamacita's offer, whatever the fuck that was. I waved off Calvin's confused look. No need to drag him into that particular mess.

When Calvin asked what I needed the money for, I explained about Joshua's budget for the new company. The kid's a whiz with numbers, and I trust his judgment. But damn, that price tag still makes me want to curl up in a ball and cry.

Then Calvin came up with the idea of more partners. He

suggested bringing in Damian, Korbin, and himself as additional investors. I'll admit, the thought of Korbin being involved made me hesitate. The guy can barely decide if he likes me or wants to kill me on any given day. Calvin assured me Korbin's not as bad as I think, just careful. And loaded.

Calvin's suggestion wasn't entirely moronic. Even a broken clock is right twice a day.

I teased Calvin, asking why I shouldn't go straight to Korbin with this golden opportunity. His puppy-dog face was almost enough to make me cave on the spot. We bantered back and forth, and I have to admit, it felt good to laugh after the stress of the past few days.

In the end, we struck a deal. Calvin, Damian, and Korbin would each buy in for four hundred and fifty thousand. It's more than Derek paid, but he took a bigger risk jumping in blind. I hope Damian and Korbin are as eager as Calvin thinks they'll be.

As Calvin and I continued talking about the business, I felt a glimmer of hope. Maybe things were getting back on track. Naturally, the universe had to throw another curveball my way.

Hope is for the weak and the foolish. As you two prattled on about percentages and investments, I longed for the days of old. Back when deals were sealed with blood and souls, not handshakes and paperwork. You modern humans have no appreciation for the art of a truly diabolical contract.

Jeremy popped his head in, reminding me about our sparring session. Shit. I'd completely lost track of time. I scrambled to change and meet him in the training center, feeling like a complete idiot for forgetting something so important.

Ooh! A prospect of some violence. Maybe I'll get to see you take a few solid hits.

As we started sparring, Jeremy mentioned learning from his last fight—moving his feet more and being okay with falling. It reminded me of my early days and how terrified I was to drop to my knees. Now it's one of my signature moves. Funny how things change.

Jeremy asked how I was so strong, and I had to bite my tongue to keep from laughing. If he only knew. I told him it was the "infected" in me, which set Pandora off on another tirade.

"I'm not a virus, Katie," she growled in my head. "You didn't catch me, and you can't Robitussin me away either."

I ignored her, focusing on Jeremy instead. I tried to explain about centering yourself and pulling from the strength inside. Pandora wasn't having it.

"I'll show you strength," she snarled. "Or maybe Hot Cheeks can. Why don't you wrestle him back in our bed and get me some ass? I mean, hell—it's been forever. Or are you still the little prude you were when I met you?"

Holy hell, sometimes I wonder if I'm living with a horny teenager instead of an ancient demon. I told her to cut it out, but she kept pushing, trying to take control of my hand. I fought back, knowing she'd probably make me grab Jeremy's junk or something equally mortifying.

While I was busy playing tug-of-war with my limbs, Jeremy saw an opening and took it. His uppercut caught me square on the chin, and suddenly I flew ass over teakettle across the floor.

The pain was intense, but Pandora's smug satisfaction pissed me off. "I don't feel bad for you at all," she said. "Just think of it this way. I'm training you, so be happy. You need to be able to take a punch, to get knocked down and work your way back from it. This was good for you."

Yeah, right. Good for me. I'll show her good later.

Jeremy was freaking out, apologizing profusely. I waved him off, trying to play it cool as my vision swam. When he checked my chin, his confusion was evident. The cut was already healing, thanks to Pandora's demonic influence. I guess that was her way of saying sorry, but it didn't make the throbbing in my head any less intense.

My moment of schadenfreude was short-lived. The accelerated healing kicked in, courtesy of yours truly. I felt a twinge of something...not guilt, mind you. Succubi don't feel guilty. It was more like professional pride. Yes, that's it. I take pride in my work, even if it involves keeping an insufferable human alive.

We got back to sparring, and I made sure to let Pandora know I accepted her apology. As much as she drives me crazy sometimes, I have to admit it's not all bad having her around. I'm not alone in this mess.

Pandora had to ruin the moment. "Knock that sentimental shit off before I make you punch yourself," she griped.

I smiled. Some things never change.

That fleeting instant akin to camaraderie makes me want to retch, but I can't deny it entirely. Your apology and admission that having me around wasn't "so bad" made me feel a warmth I quickly suppressed.

Looking back on this rollercoaster of a day, I'm exhausted but oddly hopeful. The money situation isn't solved yet, but we have a plan. My training is progressing, even if it means taking a few hits along the way. As for Pandora...she's still a pain in the ass, but she's *my* pain in the ass.

Tomorrow's another day, another chance to kick some demon ass and maybe get a step closer to figuring out this whole infected demon hunter gig. For now, I'm going to drag my bruised body to bed and pray for a dreamless sleep.

Here's hoping tomorrow brings fewer punches to the face and more answers.

You might be a prude with a hero complex, but you're not entirely useless. Your combat skills are improving, and your determination is admirable in a pathetic human kind of way.

Don't get me wrong. I still hate this situation with every fiber of my being. I long for the day when I can break free and wreak havoc on this miserable world. Until then, I suppose there are worse hosts I could be stuck with.

Who knows? Maybe your business venture will lead to some interesting opportunities for chaos and destruction. If I happen to keep you alive and somewhat functional while I wait for the perfect moment to strike, well, that's just good strategy. A dead host is of no use to anyone.

CHAPTER EIGHTEEN

Another day, another fucking crisis. Sometimes I think the universe is waiting to drop a steaming pile of shit on our heads every time we start to feel remotely comfortable. This morning started normal enough. I got up early, threw on some clothes, and made a beeline for the coffee pot.

There was something in the air, a feeling I couldn't shake. It's like that moment before a storm hits when the air gets heavy, and you can taste the electricity. I had and hated that feeling even before I got Damned. It's like my body's personal alarm system, warning me that shit's about to hit the fan.

I tried to shake it off, telling myself it was paranoia from all the crap we've been dealing with lately. As I stood there sipping my coffee and staring out the dew-covered window, that knot in my stomach wouldn't go away. Should've known better than to ignore my instincts.

Nice melancholic poet portrayal, squinting out the window like that. As for "something in the air?" It's called impending doom, and even a half-wit succubus could sense it. Next time pay attention when I try to make you feel the dread in the pit of your stomach.

Sure enough, Korbin's voice blared over the loudspeaker, calling everyone to the kitchen. Something was up since he didn't do his usual military-style repeat. He flipped on those damn red lights and left us hanging. By the time everyone stumbled in, looking various shades of confused and annoyed, I practically vibrated with nervous energy.

Korbin finally graced us with his presence, and boy, did he have some news for us. Intel suggests a major city is about to get hit. Fan-fucking-tastic. To add insult to injury, they don't know where it will happen.

The color drained from Calvin's face as he muttered about how similar this sounded to the last big attack. Yeah, no shit Sherlock. Only this time, it's supposed to be "tactical" and "specific." Because that makes it so much better, right?

Gee, it's almost like the demons have a playbook or something. And "tactical?" Oh joy, you humans are in for a treat.

As Korbin laid out the possibilities—a church, a hospital, or something bigger—the tension in the room ratcheted up. Eric hit the nail on the head when he pointed out we probably didn't have much time. No fucking kidding. The higher-ups are scrambling and pulling in extra hands, but it feels like too little, too late. We'll get caught with our pants down, and it'll be a bloodbath.

Korbin thinks it'll be multiple spots. Give the man a cookie. It's not like demons have been using that strategy since the dawn of time or anything. You humans act like you're the first to ever face an other-

worldly threat. News flash: We've been doing this dance since before your ancestors crawled out of the primordial ooze.

The best part? They're "gaming the odds" on the West Coast. California, to be precise. Because demons always follow human logic, right? It's not like we have millennia of experience in misdirection or anything. But sure, focus all your resources on one spot. That'll end well.

Korbin looked at Jeremy and me, acknowledging "the punch." Landing that blow might've boosted Jeremy's confidence, but I nodded in agreement when Korbin told us to keep the beatdowns to a minimum. Can't have the boss thinking I'm going soft or anything.

Then Korbin listed three possible scenarios, each worse than the last. One big incursion, two large ones, or multiple strikes carried out simultaneously. Calvin wasn't wrong when he said it was the stuff of nightmares. My heart raced as I considered the implications. If it's one strike, we go in guns blazing. Two, we split up and pray we're enough. If it's multiple, we're royally fucked without backup.

As the meeting broke up, the weight settled on everyone's shoulders. This is why we're here, why we do what we do, but damn if it doesn't feel overwhelming sometimes. Korbin asked Calvin and me to stay behind, probably hoping for some brilliant insight. Pandora chimed in with her two cents.

"Multiple incursions, same location," she said. "Trying for a major infestation." I wanted to tell her to fuck off with her cryptic bullshit, but something in her tone made me pause. She wouldn't put herself at risk unless she was damn sure. As much as I hate to admit it, we need all the intel we can get right now.

I shared Pandora's hunch with Korbin and Calvin, careful to frame it as my intuition. Calvin accepted it without question. Determination and dread filled me as we hashed out strategies.

We're talking about calling in favors, deploying extra teams, and basically putting all our eggs in one very fragile basket.

The three of you playing at being generals was painful to watch. You think you're so clever, planning deployments and calling in reinforcements. You might as well be children playing chess, believing you're masters of strategy when you can barely move the piece correctly.

The conversation shifted to the business, and I explained the financial situation to Korbin. Over a million dollars. Jesus Christ, when did my life become about juggling demon invasions and startup costs? Calvin's idea of bringing in more investors seemed solid, but I wasn't prepared for Korbin's curveball.

Eight-point-seven-five million dollars. For the whole company. I'd be lying if I said I wasn't tempted. For a split second, I saw flashes of the life I used to dream about—financial security, the chance to build something truly mine, a future without constant fear and violence. Then reality crashed back in. What future? I'm Damned, for fuck's sake. I don't know if I'll be alive next week, let alone long enough to build an empire.

I looked at Calvin's hopeful face and knew I couldn't do it. This company, as insane as it is, means something to all of us. It's our little slice of normalcy in a world gone mad. I turned Korbin down, sticking to the original plan of ten percent for $450,000. The relief on Calvin's face was worth more than any amount of money Korbin could have offered.

I almost respect you for turning down Korbin's offer. Then you went and sold thirty percent for a pittance.

As I left to talk to Joshua—poor bastard's probably going stir-crazy at Mamacita's—I had mixed emotions. Pride in what we're building, fear of what's coming, and a strange contentment. We might be facing hell on Earth, but we'll face it together.

I wonder what Calvin, Damian, and Korbin discussed after I left. Probably more business bullshit. Or maybe they bet on how long it'll take before I snap and deck someone. My money's on Pandora being the next target. That demon bitch is getting on my last nerve with her cryptic warnings and half-truths.

Speaking of Pandora, I can't shake the feeling that she knows more than she's letting on about this upcoming attack. Why is she suddenly so helpful? What's her angle? I'd love nothing more than to exorcise her ass out of my head, but right now, we need every advantage we can get. Even if it means dealing with her smug, demonic presence.

You should try it from my perspective. Having no choice except to watch and occasionally whisper in your ear is maddening. I've led armies, toppled empires, and seduced kings. Now I'm reduced to watching incompetent humans bumble through a war they can't possibly understand.

All I can do is bide my time. Every demon knows patience is a virtue, ironically enough.

What the hell have I gotten myself into? I'm strategizing about demon invasions, running a weapons manufacturing company, and trying to save the world. If someone had told me a year ago that this would be my life, I'd have laughed in their face and suggested they lay off the drugs.

Tomorrow, we'll start preparing for whatever hellish scenario is coming our way. We'll train harder, plan smarter, and do whatever it takes to keep this world from falling into demon hands. But tonight? Tonight, I'm going to pour myself a stiff drink and try to remember what it feels like to be normal. Even if it's only for a few hours.

Who knows? Maybe I'll dream about that beach Korbin

mentioned—sun, sand, and not a demon in sight. A girl can dream, right?

CHAPTER NINETEEN

Katie's Journal

Another day in this hellish nightmare I call my life. I woke up to the sound of trucks and machinery outside my window, and for a split second, I thought I was back in my old life. You know, the one where demons and impending doom didn't constantly surround me. Nope, just another day in the life of Katie, the reluctant savior of humanity. Yay me.

I stumbled out of bed, feeling like a truck hit me. These nightmares are taking their toll. Every time I close my eyes, I see the faces of the people I've lost, the battles we've fought, and the horrors that are yet to come. It's fucking exhausting.

Your subconscious fears can't compare to the hellish reality I've endured.

As I looked out the window, I couldn't believe my eyes. There were trucks everywhere, people bustling around, and it looked like a construction site had exploded in our backyard. What the hell was going on? I threw on some clothes and raced downstairs, my heart pounding. The last thing I needed was some bigwig breathing down my neck about unauthorized activity.

The scene outside was pure chaos. Men carried equipment, trucks moved in and out, and Joshua looked like a kid on Christmas morning in the middle of it all. I have to admit, seeing him so excited made me smile. It was nice to see someone genuinely happy in this mess we're in.

A veritable circus of trucks and burly men swarmed the area, transforming the building into a hive of activity. Watching you stumble around like a newborn fawn in your normal state of perpetual bewilderment, narrowly avoiding being trampled by the workers, was almost comical.

I spotted a familiar face as I dodged workers and equipment to make my way through the crowd. It took me a moment to place her, but then it hit me. She was one of the girls from the brothel. And she wasn't the only one. They were everywhere, dressed in normal clothes, working alongside the men. It was surreal.

I finally reached Joshua, and he was practically bouncing with excitement. "It's great, isn't it?" He beamed. I wanted to be mad. I really did. He'd gone behind my back and started all this without my approval. After seeing the joy on his face, I couldn't bring myself to burst his bubble.

"Um, yeah," I managed to say, still trying to process everything. "But Joshua, where did you get all of this? I didn't give you the extra budget yet."

His response floored me. He'd put the down payments on his account, trusting I'd come through with the money later. The faith this guy has in me is touching and terrifying. I'm not used to people believing in me like that, and it's a lot of pressure.

The boy wonder commanded this impromptu army with surprising authority. It was a refreshing change from his usual timid demeanor. Perhaps there's more to him than meets the eye. Still, his eagerness to please you is nauseating.

Mamacita appeared out of nowhere as if the day couldn't get any weirder. Seeing her here, in this context, was like having two completely different worlds collide. She explained that Joshua had offered the girls from the brothel a "stupid amount of money" to help with the cleanup. My first instinct was to be pissed. This wasn't exactly the kind of job you hired casual workers for. Mamacita quickly set me straight.

"I didn't take any of it. Not one cent," she said, hands up in surrender. "I did offer an appropriate amount of money to some of the ladies to help with whatever they needed in their lives. The ones that knew Joshua was your boy decided they would do some vertical work for a while."

I admit seeing the girls looking so normal and happy was a shock. They were smiling, working hard, and seemed genuinely excited to be there. It made me wonder about their lives, about the choices they'd made or had forced upon them. In a weird way, I felt a kinship with them. We're all just trying to make the best of the hand we've been dealt, aren't we?

Oh, the irony of seeing these women dressed like ordinary laborers instead of dolled up and scantily clad. Your shock was palpable, and I reveled in your discomfort. It's about time you faced the reality of the world you stumbled into.

Mamacita is an opportunist. She wasted no time in explaining how she facilitated this little arrangement. I'll give credit where it's due. This woman knows how to play her cards. She helped her girls while maintaining a façade of altruism. It's almost admirable in a devious sort of way.

I made my way back to Joshua, who was practically drooling over some new equipment. As much as I wanted to be annoyed with him for going behind my back, I admired his enthusiasm and initiative. When I asked him about the timeline for new weapons, his answer was exciting and disappointing.

"Three weeks for our first knife?" he said, looking thoughtful. "After that, though, I should be putting out at least one knife or sword a week, minimum. I gotta get used to the equipment and such first."

I tried not to let my disappointment show. I hoped for faster results, but I had to remind myself that quality takes time. If these weapons will keep us alive in future battles, I want them to be perfect.

When I thought the day couldn't get more emotional, Joshua pulled out a gold cross. "I have this," he said, nodding at one of the girls. "I want you to give it to Damian. Jules says he helped her one time, and she hoped he didn't die doing whatever it was that he did."

The lump in my throat caught me off guard. These little reminders of the humanity in the people around me, of the connections we forge even in the darkest times, hit me hard. I accepted the cross, thinking about Damian and how much this would mean to him.

"Thank you, Joshua," I managed to say, my voice thick with emotion. "I don't want him to die either. You will come to find out that though we are the Damned, we are a special breed. We take family seriously, and thus take our teams seriously because they are the only ones we have in this world."

The pièce de résistance of this farcical day was Joshua's grand reveal of his progress. Three weeks for a single knife? I've seen glaciers move faster. Yet you nodded like an obedient puppy while trying to mask your disappointment. If this is the best humanity has to offer in terms of weaponry against demonic forces, we might as well surrender now and save ourselves the embarrassment.

But wait, there was more! Joshua produced a golden cross for Damian. Talk about a moment of misguided sentimentality. As if a piece of shiny metal could protect anyone from the horrors that await us. It took every ounce of my willpower not to make you vomit on the spot due to your sickeningly sweet gratitude and team spirit.

I reflected on how much my life has changed as Joshua walked away. Here I am, surrounded by ex-prostitutes turned construction workers, a genius weapons maker who trusts me implicitly, and a looming battle that could determine the fate of humanity. Somehow, we're forging connections, building trust, and finding moments of joy amid this chaos and danger.

I allow myself to feel a glimmer of hope, but I can't shake the dread building in the pit of my stomach. The nightmares that plague my sleep aren't random fears. They're warnings. Something big is coming, and I'm not sure we're ready for it.

I think about the demon I saw in my dreams last night, the one standing on the balcony overlooking a hellish landscape. His words echo in my mind. "Soon I will have another domain to play with. There will be even more slaves to feed my conquest. More souls to claim, more demons to scatter about."

The thought of that monster and his plans for our world makes my blood boil. I've seen too much and lost too many people to let that happen. But how the hell am I supposed to stop it? I'm one person, albeit with some freaky demon powers I still don't fully understand.

Then there's Pandora. That cryptic bitch has been suspiciously quiet lately, which never bodes well. I can't shake the feeling that she's playing a long game and I'm a pawn in her cosmic chess match. But what choice do I have but to play along?

She's the only one with any answers, even if she doles them out like they're precious gems.

Despite my contempt for mortals and your pitiful attempts at preparation, I'm grudgingly invested in your survival. Not out of any sense of affection, mind you, but out of sheer self-preservation. If you die, so do I. And I'll be damned if I let some low-ranking demon or half-wit human be the end of me.

We're on the precipice of a battle that will determine the fate of this realm. Our assets are a weapons maker who works at a snail's pace, a reformed madam and her flock of ex-prostitutes, and a ragtag team of humans with more bravado than brains. It's enough to make the most optimistic soul question the odds.

Perhaps that's the beauty of it all. You humans push forward in blissful ignorance, driven by a hope that borders on delusion. It's infuriating and fascinating. Part of me wants to see you fail spectacularly if only to prove the futility of your efforts. Another part I'm loath to acknowledge wonders if your stubborn determination might be enough to tip the scales in your favor.

The absurdity of my past versus my present strikes me as I stand here watching the hustle and bustle around me. I'm preparing for a war against demons, trying to master powers I never asked for, and leading a team against forces we barely understand.

Part of me wants to laugh, another part wants to cry, and a small, traitorous part wants to run away and never look back. I can't. I won't. These people are counting on me. As terrifying as that is, it also keeps me going.

I don't know what tomorrow will bring, but I won't go down without a fight. That demon lord and his minions might think they have the upper hand, but they haven't met me and my band of misfits yet.

Bring it on, you scaly bastards. We're ready for you.

Well, almost ready. First, I need a drink and about twelve hours of uninterrupted sleep. A girl's gotta have priorities, right?

I ponder our predicament as night falls and you finally settle into an uneasy sleep. Will Joshua's weapons be the game-changer we need? Can your band of misfits and outcasts truly stand against the forces of Hell? Or are we all pawns in a cosmic game, destined to be sacrificed for some greater purpose?

Only time will tell. If we do go down, I'll ensure we do it in a blaze of glory the devil himself will remember for eternity.

CHAPTER TWENTY

Katie's Journal

What a fucking day. It all started when I dragged my ass upstairs after another grueling training session. I swear, if I have to do one more set of burpees, I might combust. I digress. There I was, panting like I'd run a marathon, when I stumbled upon the guys looking dapper and ready to head out.

Damian was in his usual shirt, tie, and long overcoat ensemble. I teased him about looking "dapper as fuck." Come on, it's not every day you see a priest channeling his inner James Bond. Derek and Eric were nearby.

I perked up faster than a cat hearing a can opener when they mentioned barbecue. Then cringed when they told me where they were going. These poor, misguided souls were about to make a grave mistake by settling for some touristy joint on the Strip. Not on my watch.

"Jesus," I blurted before realizing I was talking to a priest. Oops. But seriously, the thought of them missing out on Jessie

Rae's was practically sacrilegious. I snatched those keys from Damian's hand faster than you can say "pulled pork." Sorry, not sorry.

The drive to Jessie Rae's was a trip down memory lane. The Vegas lights blurred by as I thought about how much my life had changed. Remember when my biggest worry was which slot machine to try next? Now I'm gearing up for a fucking demon invasion. Talk about a career change.

As we pulled up to a tiny strip mall, I could practically taste the smoky goodness already. Derek had the audacity to question where they smoked their meat. I nearly smacked him upside the head. "Shut your mouth!" I quipped, probably a bit too aggressively. But come on, questioning Jessie Rae's? Those are fighting words.

Inside, the smell hit us like a delicious, meaty tidal wave. If heaven has a scent, I swear it's Jessie Rae's barbecue. I reminisced about the last time I was here with my friends as we waited in line. It felt like a lifetime ago—before demons, before training, before my whole world turned upside down.

The smell in that hole-in-the-wall joint was enough to make me wish for the sweet release of exorcism. But no, I had to endure the full experience.

I made damn sure everyone knew about the waffle fries. "If you don't try them, you're an idiot," I declared. I wasn't joking about regrowing fingers if they dared touch mine. A girl's gotta have boundaries, especially when it comes to waffle fries.

While we waited for our food, I dug deeper into Eric's demon fascination. I mean, the guy wants a demon. Talk about daddy issues. When I suggested helping him find one, he looked at me like I'd grown a second head. Oh, sweet summer child. If he only knew what I was capable of.

We sat there surrounded by the unwashed masses, and you gave him demon acquisition advice like it's a fucking pet adoption. Never mind the irony of doing it with a succubus of unparalleled power trapped inside you.

Eric was a pillock, bragging about his "virile manhood" being too much for an incubus. I hate to break it to him, but I've seen more impressive specimens on medieval peasants during the Black Death. Human arrogance never ceases to amaze me.

The conversation took an interesting turn when I brought up the possibility of a succubus. You should've seen their faces! Eric turned redder than the BBQ sauce, and Damian suddenly found the ceiling fascinating. Men, I swear.

It hit me like a ton of bricks—these guys probably needed a "knock before entering" policy. Even Damian, Mr. "I'm a priest" himself. Yeah, right. I've seen how he looks at me when he thinks I'm not paying attention.

Ha! Their expressions when you suggested a succubus were priceless! You'd have thought Caligula walked in and proposed an orgy. The awkward silence was almost worth the torment of being there.

As we dug into our food—those waffle fries were orgasmic, by the way—a strange sense of normalcy washed over me. For a moment, we weren't demon hunters, chosen ones, or whatever the hell we are. We were friends, enjoying some damn good barbecue and each other's company.

Reality has a way of creeping back in, doesn't it? Later that night, I stared at the cross Joshua had given me. It was meant for Damian, a "weapon fit for a priest," as I put it. Handing it over felt like more than gifting a trinket. It felt like acknowledging the danger we're all in.

I wrapped that cross in satin and tied it with a ribbon, trying to make it look less like the potential lifesaver it was and more like a normal gift. When I knocked on Damian's door—see, I'm learning—he looked genuinely surprised. I guess demon hunters aren't big on the whole gift-giving thing.

Watching Damian unwrap that cross was intense. The way his eyes lit up, you'd think I'd handed him the Holy Grail. His expression changed when I explained its true purpose was to be used against demons. That kind, priestly demeanor melted away, replaced by something darker and more determined. It was a stark reminder of who Damian is beneath the collar and the charm.

Playing Santa Claus? Really? I guess every priest needs a gift that reminds them of their impending mortality.

I could have done without Damian's sentimental drivel before he focused on doing his job. I'm not sure how many demons his shiny new toy will smite. Such trinkets are ineffective against beings like me.

I couldn't shake my feeling of unease as I left his room. We're gearing up for war, aren't we? Against forces we barely understand. Yet here I am, cracking jokes about waffle fries and succubi. Sometimes I wonder if I'm cut out for this shit.

Then I remember the alternative. A world overrun by demons, where nights full of laughter, barbecue, and friends like tonight are nothing but a distant memory. I know I have to keep fighting, training, and pushing myself to be stronger, faster, smarter.

At the end of the day, what choice do we have? We're the thin line between humanity and Hell itself. If that means I have to sacrifice my normal life, my safety, maybe my sanity... Well, bring it on.

Still, I wonder about the others. Derek, with his memes and his Southern barbecue cravings. Eric, with his misplaced confidence and soap opera addiction. And Damian...oh, Damian. The priest who's not quite as saintly as he'd like us to believe. We're a ragtag bunch, that's for sure. Maybe that's our strength. We're unpredictable and unconventional. The demons won't know what hit them.

Speaking of demons, I still can't wrap my head around Eric's fascination with them. When I suggested he might end up with a succubus, the look on his face was priceless. I mean, come on, dude. Be careful what you wish for. A succubus might sound fun in theory, but I've seen what these creatures can do. It's not pretty.

Then there's Damian. The way he clutched that cross, the fire in his eyes...it was like seeing a completely different person. Sometimes I forget that beneath all the priestly charm is a warrior who's dedicated his life to fighting evil. It's inspiring and terrifying.

I wonder what the others think about all this. Do they lie awake at night, like I do, wondering if we're ready for what's coming? Do they second-guess their decisions and abilities? Or am I the only one plagued by doubt?

God, I miss my old life sometimes. The simplicity of it all. Wake up, go to classes, maybe hit the casino on the weekend. No demons, no training, no impending apocalypse hanging over my head. Then I think about what's at stake and all the innocent people who have no idea what's coming for them. I can't walk away, even if I wanted to.

Tomorrow, it's back to training. Back to preparing for a war that most of the world doesn't even know is coming. But tonight? Tonight, I'll savor the lingering taste of that barbecue, the memory of laughter shared with friends, and pretend for a little while that we're normal people living normal lives.

Because who knows? This might be the last bit of normalcy we get for a long, long time.

Shit, I'm getting maudlin. Maybe I should've had another beer with that barbecue. Or perhaps I should raid Damian's not-so-secret whiskey stash. After all, what's he gonna do? Excommunicate me?

Nah, better not. Gotta keep a clear head. The demons aren't going to exorcise themselves, after all.

Here's hoping tomorrow brings more laughter than danger. But if it doesn't? Well, bring it on, hellspawn. This barbecue-loving, waffle fry-defending badass is ready for you.

Note to self: Find out if holy water works on hangovers. You know, for science.

Reflecting on this day reminds me of why I despise humanity so much. Their petty concerns, laughable attempts at camaraderie, and delusions of grandeur are all so utterly pointless. They strut around like peacocks, oblivious to the true powers that lurk in the shadows.

In the end, when all is said and done and I stand victorious over your broken bodies, maybe I'll treat myself to some of that barbecue you're so fond of. After all, a succubus deserves a little indulgence now and then.

CHAPTER TWENTY-ONE

Katie's Journal

The morning started like any other. We were all gathered around the table, half alive and desperately clinging to our caffeine lifelines. I nursed my coffee, trying to shake off the fog of sleep while eyeing the others. Pandora was unusually quiet, probably still sulking about our new weapons venture. For an ancient demon, she can be such a drama queen sometimes.

Your morning routine is as dull as watching paint dry in Pompeii. Coffee, bagels, and mindless chatter. It's enough to make a succubus wish for eternal slumber. Also, I'm not sulking. I'm biding my time. You have no idea what's brewing beneath the surface.

Korbin was MIA, likely stuck on another bullshit conference call with the higher-ups. Poor bastard, having to deal with all the political crap on top of keeping us in line. I don't envy him one bit.

After finishing my coffee, I headed to my room to pull on and lace up my boots. I looked out the window and spotted Joshua scurrying into the other building. I giggled at his perfectly tucked shirt and those ridiculous brown pants. Does he own anything else? Maybe I should buy him a Hawaiian shirt for his birthday to see if he would spontaneously combust.

My amusement was short-lived. Red lights flashed, the siren blared, and my stomach dropped. Fuck. This was it—the real deal. I didn't wait for an announcement. I grabbed my knives and bolted for the training area. My heart was pounding so hard I thought it might burst from my chest.

Those red lights are like a tacky disco inferno. Just saying. The lot of you scrambling like ants whose hill got kicked was pathetic, but the surge of adrenaline was invigorating.

When Korbin finally showed up for the briefing, the tension in the room was thick enough to cut with one of my blades. He whispered something to Damian, and Damian's hand instinctively went to his new cross. Whatever was going down, it was bad.

"A bus full of children is missing in Los Angeles," Korbin announced. My blood ran cold. Those sick fucks. Of all the low-down, dirty tricks they could pull, they had to go after kids. I wanted to scream and punch something, but I held it together. Barely.

As Korbin laid out the possibilities of terrorists or a major demon incursion, Pandora stirred inside me. She was focused, almost eager, and it made me uneasy. What did she know that we didn't?

You're all so convinced it's demons or terrorists. Humans and your need to categorize evil. As if the lines between monster and man aren't blurred beyond recognition.

We suited up in record time, a well-oiled machine of controlled chaos. I made sure to grab Eric's preferred guns for him while he focused on his medic gear. The guy's a lifesaver, and I'll be damned if I let him go into battle unprepared.

The ride to the airport and the flight to LA were a blur of nervous energy and silent prayers. I kept thinking about those kids, imagining the terror they must feel. It made me sick to my stomach, but it fueled my determination. We would find them and make those demon bastards pay.

When we landed at Bob Hope Airport, the reality of the situation hit me like a ton of bricks. This wasn't a training exercise or a small-time demon hunt. This was the big leagues, and the stakes couldn't be higher.

Korbin split us into three teams, and I led Team Three with Damian and Eric. Part of me was thrilled at the responsibility, but another part was scared shitless. These were my friends and family, and their lives were in my hands.

I almost pity your group and the others for walking into this blind.

I felt the sickness spreading through the city as we headed to our designated spot near Disneyland. Talk about irony. It was a new sensation that made my skin crawl and my stomach churn. Pandora was unusually quiet, but I sensed her anticipation.

I snapped at her in my mind, "I don't know what you know, Pandora, but if this is some kind of trap, I swear I'll slit my own damn throat and drag you down to Hell kicking and screaming."

Her response was simple. "I know." Then silence. Great, just what I needed—a cryptic demon riding shotgun in my head.

Your threat was entertaining. As if you could truly drag me to Hell. Sweet, foolish Katie. You have no idea what hell is.

We pulled into an abandoned parking lot, and I laid down the law for my team. No bullshit, no showboating, and absolutely no demon-hunting side quests. This was about saving lives and taking out as many of those bastards as we could.

Then we waited. God, the waiting was the worst part. My mind kept conjuring horrific scenarios, each one worse than the last. What if we were too late? What if the kids were already... No, I couldn't let myself go there.

Hours ticked by, and still nothing. The tension built in our team and across the city. It was the calm before a storm, the eerie stillness that makes the hairs on your nape stand up.

When Calvin's team finally got the call, my heart leapt into my throat. The shit was about to hit the fan. Part of me was relieved we weren't first up, but another part itched to get into the fight.

As we listened to Calvin's team head out, I couldn't shake the feeling that this was only the beginning. Whatever was coming would be big and ugly.

I looked at Damian and Eric, my teammates and friends. We were in this together, come hell or high water. Knowing our luck, probably both. I silently promised myself I'd do whatever it took to get them through this alive.

The waiting continued, and each second felt like an eternity. My mind raced with possibilities, strategies, and worst-case scenarios. I kept checking my weapons, a nervous habit that gave my hands something to do.

Pandora's presence in my mind was a constant reminder of the bizarre reality we were living in. Here I was, a demon hunter with a demon of my own, about to face God knows what in the City of Angels. The irony wasn't lost on me.

You realize this is absurd, right? You humans play at being heroes but have no idea of the cosmic forces at work.

Your determination is admirable, in a way. You believe you can make a difference and save lives. It's almost tragic how misguided you are.

The truth is, the world is far darker and more complex than any of you realize. Demons, humans, good, evil—they're meaningless labels in the grand scheme of things. There are powers at play that would shatter fragile human minds if you even glimpsed them.

I thought about the kids on that bus, imagining their fear and confusion. It made my blood boil. No child should have to face the horrors we deal with. I swore to myself that we'd find and save them. If any demon had so much as touched a hair on their heads, I'd personally ensure they experienced a whole new level of hell.

As the night wore on, I reflected on how I'd ended up here. From a normal life to hunting demons, leading a team, carrying one of the Seventy-Two inside me. It was insane and terrifying, yet I couldn't imagine doing anything else. This was my purpose, my calling. Despite the danger and fear, I knew I was exactly where I needed to be.

I glanced at Damian with his hand still resting on his new cross. I wondered what was going through his mind. A priest turned demon hunter. Talk about a career change. And Eric, our medic, ready to patch us up and jump back into the fray. We were an odd bunch, that's for sure, but there was no one else I'd rather have by my side.

I'm torn between anticipation and disdain as we sit here waiting. Part of me wants to see how this plays out, to watch as your illusions of control and righteousness crumble around you. Another part of me longs to break free and show you what true power looks like.

For now, I'll wait. You and your teammates can have your little adven-

ture and think you're making a difference. It won't matter in the end. The wheels are already in motion. Not even your precious faith or determination can stop what's coming.

The silence was broken by Korbin's voice in our earpieces, checking in. No change in status. Still waiting. His words echoed in my head. "This will happen." The certainty in his voice was reassuring and terrifying.

Then Calvin's team got their call. An abandoned store, a cop down, another missing. As they headed out, we wished them luck, but the words felt hollow. Luck had nothing to do with what we were about to face.

As silence fell again, I wondered when our turn would come. What horrors would we find? How many innocents would we be able to save? How many of us would make it out alive?

The weight of leadership felt heavier than ever. These people trusted me with their lives, and I was determined not to let them down. We were more than a team. We were family. And family looks out for each other, no matter what.

So here we sit in this godforsaken parking lot, waiting for hell to break loose. My nerves are shot, my adrenaline is pumping, and Pandora is stirring restlessly inside me. Whatever's coming, we'll face it head-on because that's what we do. We're demon hunters, we're warriors, and we're the only thing standing between humanity and the forces of Hell.

Oh, Katie. Your bravery and conviction are futile given what you're up against. I'll give you this. You amaze me with your capacity for hope in the face of overwhelming odds. It doesn't change the fact that all your plans and preparations will mean nothing in the face of what's coming.

I almost feel sorry for you.

Bring it on, you demonic bastards. We're ready for you.

The show is about to begin, and I have a front-row seat to the chaos. Let's see how long your resolve lasts when you face true horror.

What the ever-loving fuck? I thought I'd seen it all, but this was something else entirely. We got the call about trouble at one of the big churches in the city, and I knew it would be bad. I had no idea how fucked up things were about to get.

A church. How predictable. These demons always go for the low-hanging fruit, don't they? Your anxiety built as we drove there. Poor little lamb, still not used to the carnage.

Tension radiated off Damian as we pulled up near the church. The recognition in his eyes when he saw that steeple was like he was staring down his personal demon. I wanted to ask him about it, but there wasn't time. We had a job to do.

I pulled out the tablet and checked the blueprints. The old stone chapel in the cemetery had a secret passage into the church. It seemed like our best bet for a stealthy entrance. Pandora stirred inside me, eager for action as I explained the plan to the guys. I told that bitch to simmer down. We needed clear heads for this.

We made our way through the cemetery, keeping low. I half expected to see zombies pop out of graves, but it was eerily quiet. When we reached the chapel, Damian and Eric cleared it while I took point. The passageway was creepy as fuck, all cobwebs and mold. I swear I felt something skitter across my foot at one point. I nearly jumped out of my skin, but I kept it together.

When we reached the end, I was surprised to discover the door was unlocked. Damian explained some bullshit about it being a symbol that the church never closes its doors. I rolled my eyes. "Always tricking people," I muttered. These religious types and their mind games, I swear.

Snicker. The church's idea of an "open door policy." Damian knew way too much about it. Ex-altar boy, perhaps?

We crept into the main hallway, and I heard the screaming inside the sanctuary. My heart pounded so hard I thought it might burst out of my chest. I took a deep breath, looked at the guys, and nodded. This was it.

Nothing could have prepared me for what we saw when we opened those doors. Bodies everywhere—in the aisles, slumped over in pews, sprawled across the altar. The smell of blood and fear was overwhelming. I froze. This wasn't just another demon attack. This was a fucking massacre.

Eric snapped me out of it by rushing forward to check for survivors. He tended to a few older ladies who'd somehow made it through the carnage. When he came back, he looked shaken to his core. I grabbed his shoulders, trying to ground him.

"I know it's hard," I whispered, fighting to keep my voice steady. "But we have to find this demon. We have to fix this. I need you to ball up all that emotion and bury it. Bury it as deep as you can until we get out of here. When we get back, we'll deal with what we've seen."

He nodded and took a deep breath. "I got this," he said, and determination returned to his eyes. Good. We needed everyone at their best for whatever hellish shit was waiting for us.

Oh, honey. If only you knew how to truly bury your emotions. I could teach you a thing or two.

Damian called me over then, pointing to one of the priests. The poor bastard held his guts in with one hand as blood poured between his fingers. But there was fire in his eyes as he looked up at me.

"Behind the holy water," he gasped. "Steps that go underground!"

I nodded, feeling Pandora surge forward. My eyes flashed red as I pulled out my pistols. "Kill that sonofabitch!" the priest yelled as we raced toward the pulpit. I glanced back just in time to see him collapse. Another life lost to this madness. I swore then and there that whatever was down those steps would pay.

The passageway was dark and damp, the air thick with the stench of evil. I swapped my pistols for my short swords, gripping them tightly. Pandora's voice echoed in my head, assuring me she was right there with me. For once, I was glad for her presence.

I growled internally, "I don't know if this is your boyfriend, but I'm going to kill this sonofabitch."

"Don't hold back," Pandora hissed. Her anger matched mine.

I had to laugh. As if you could do it without me.

As we reached the bottom, I peered into the room ahead. Seven demons dragged bodies around like ragdolls, and their leader stood in the center. He wasn't the biggest I'd faced, but something about him made my skin crawl.

"Is it him?" I asked Pandora silently.

"No," she spat. "Just one of his cronies."

"Fuck it," I muttered. I was done with stealth. I kicked the door open and charged in, screaming like a banshee.

The big demon smiled like I was some cute little girl playing dress-up. "So cute." He chuckled. "She seeks to hurt with her little metal knives."

Oh, how wrong he was. The moment my blade sliced across his arm, his smug grin turned to a howl of agony. Joshua's weapons packed one hell of a punch against these bastards.

I didn't give him time to recover. I latched onto a tapestry behind him, using it to launch myself onto his shoulders. As I brought my knees down hard, I caught Eric's eye and winked. Then I went to work.

I ran my swords up the demon's back, savoring his roars of pain as he fell forward. "You don't deserve to die fast, you fucking bastard," I snarled, stabbing him again and again. "You deserve to suffer."

I crossed my arms and sliced through the skin on the back of his neck, scissor-style. The beast thrashed wildly, trying to throw me off, but I held on tight. I caught Damian's eye and nodded as an evil smile spread across my face.

Damian got the message. He rushed over, shouting bible verses as he pressed his weapon against the demon's head. I watched in fascination as the cross melted into the creature's skull. With one final, ear-splitting shriek, the demon collapsed and burst into dust.

You have some moves. Even I was impressed when you jumped onto that big demon's back. Not that I'd ever tell you that.

I picked myself up and looked at the remaining demons. They stared at us with what I can only describe as fear. Good. They should be afraid. Because at that moment, as I stood there covered in demon dust and my sweat, I knew we were the scariest things in the room.

I laughed. Here we were, three humans facing down a pack of hellspawn, and we were the ones with the predatory grins. "Who's next?" I called while twirling my swords.

These demons are pathetic, like overgrown toddlers throwing tantrums. Back in my day, we had real demons. Creatures that could make empires crumble with a whisper. These modern abominations? They're not fit to lick the boots of the weakest imp I used to command.

Don't even get me started on their tactics. Attacking a church? How cliché. If they want to cause chaos, they should hit where it hurts. The stock exchange, perhaps. Or better yet, a politician's mistress. Now that would be entertainment.

The fight that followed was a blur of blood, dust, and unholy screams. Damian's new weapon proved devastatingly effective, melting through demon flesh like it was butter. Eric had found his groove, moving with a grace I hadn't seen before as he took down demon after demon.

Me? I was in my element. Pandora and I were in perfect sync, our movements fluid and deadly. With each demon that fell, I felt a surge of savage joy. This is what I was made for. This is why I survived everything life had thrown at me.

When it was over, we stood in silence for a moment, catching our breath. The room was thick with demon dust, and the metallic tang of blood hung heavy in the air. I looked at my team, seeing the same exhaustion and exhilaration on their faces.

"Well," I said, breaking the silence. "I guess that's one way to clear out a church basement."

Damian let out a surprised laugh, and Eric cracked a smile.

The tension broke, and suddenly we were all laughing, probably a bit hysterically. But fuck it, we'd earned it.

Speaking of entertainment, watching you and the boys take down those demons was almost worth being trapped in this mortal coil. The way you smiled as you tortured the big one...there might be hope for you yet. A little nudge here and there, and who knows? You might make a decent succubus someday.

I digress. As the literal dust settled—these demons have no style in death —I wondered about the bigger picture. Who's pulling the strings? This feels like small potatoes compared to what's brewing. I can sense it, even if you can't. A storm is coming, and these skirmishes are only the first raindrops.

Reality sank in as we made our way back up to the sanctuary. The bodies were still there, a stark reminder of why we do this job. A wave of nausea hit me, but I pushed it down. There'd be time to process all this later.

We checked in with the survivors, ensured they were being cared for, and headed out. As we drove away from the church, I thought about how close we'd come to losing everything. One wrong move, one moment of hesitation, and we could have ended up like those poor bastards in the pews.

We didn't. We fought, we survived, and we sent a bunch of demons back to Hell where they belong. It's not much in the grand scheme of things, but it's something. Sometimes, something is enough.

The moment you realize how deep this rabbit hole goes will be delicious. Until then, I'll keep whispering suggestions and nudging you in the right direction. It's a delicate dance, influencing without revealing too much. Then again, I've always been an excellent dancer.

The adrenaline is finally wearing off. My hands are shaking, and I know the nightmares will be brutal tonight. But you know what? I'm still here. Still fighting. And tomorrow, we'll do it all over again.

Because that's the job. That's what we signed up for, despite how fucked up it is.

I felt your exhaustion. If only you knew how to tap into your potential. The power that lies dormant in you is intoxicating. One day, perhaps you'll embrace it fully. Heaven help anyone who stands in our way on that day.

For now, it's back to the mundane. Cleanup, debriefings, strategy meetings, and endless cups of that swill you call coffee and tea. How I long for the days of real stimulants. A good old-fashioned orgy would do wonders for morale, but I doubt you would go for that suggestion.

CHAPTER TWENTY-THREE

I stood in the doorway of that church, staring at the carnage before me. Bodies were everywhere. The elderly ladies we saved were the only survivors in the entire goddamn building. Even the priest didn't make it. He died in a pool of his own blood, for Christ's sake. The irony wasn't lost on me.

The only "success" we had was killing a bunch of demons, including one nasty bastard that was bigger than the rest. Small fucking consolation. No one on our team died, but Damian and I were pretty torn up. I glanced at my arm and cringed at the sight of blood trickling down to my elbow. My lip had been busted too, but that had already healed. The dried blood on my chin was a lovely reminder.

You look like you went ten rounds with a meat grinder, but your split lip healed faster than you can say "demonic regeneration."

Damian... God, he looked so broken. He sat in a chair, staring at the bodies strewn across the floor. The sadness in his eyes was gut-wrenching. He was so far gone he didn't even flinch as Eric stitched him up. I've never seen him like that before. It scared me more than I'd like to admit.

The brooding slab of man-meat has a high pain threshold. Maybe there's hope for him yet. As for Eric, let's just say he's in for a rude awakening.

When Eric finished with Damian, I limped over and plopped down in a chair. Eric cleaned my wound and shook his head. I tried to lighten the mood, asking, "What?" with a smile. He replied that he wasn't sure if he could stitch me up before it healed. "I'll give it a couple stitches for good luck," he said, his exhaustion evident.

As Eric worked in silence, I noticed the scene was getting to him. I took a deep breath and looked at Damian, who raised an eyebrow at me. I smirked, trying to keep it together. When Eric finished, I nodded my thanks.

Then I had an idea. "I was thinking," I said to Damian. "How about a Level-Four Nightmare?"

Damian nodded, agreeing it was a good choice. Poor Eric looked confused as hell, asking if it was some fancy name for a high-level bad dream. I chuckled. "Dream? Uh, no, but not a bad guess."

As Eric cleaned the last of the blood off my elbow, I reached down and tilted his head toward mine. Our eyes met, and I said, "Welcome to the infected," before parting my lips.

I slowly breathed out, releasing the last demon that had been gibbering in fear of Pandora deep inside me. The little fucker flew out of my body and straight into Eric. He shut his mouth quickly, hiccupped once, looked at me with wide eyes, and collapsed unconscious.

Pandora's voice echoed in my head. "You're welcome, Eric." I swear, she's gotten this demon-snagging shit down to a science. Damian shook his head and laughed, saying, "Gets 'em every time." Guilt twinged in my gut, but hey, better Eric than some unsuspecting civilian, right?

Gifting him a demon was a moment of brilliance no doubt inspired by yours truly. Oh, the delicious irony! The poor, clueless medic had no idea what hit him. One minute he was cleaning blood off your elbow. The next he was unconscious on the floor with a demon riding shotgun in his soul. You're welcome, Eric. Consider it a crash course in demonology.

I've perfected the art of demon-snagging. Think of it as fishing, except I use fear and desperation as bait instead of worms. That last little bugger practically begged to escape my clutches. As if any place is safe from me. Foolish creature.

The rest of the day was a blur. I was emotionally and physically drained from the op and its cleanup by the time we got back to base.

The debriefings were rough. The other teams also walked into scenes straight out of horror movies.

Calvin, Jeremy, and Rob had to deal with people strung up like fucking Christmas ornaments, blood everywhere, and demons foaming at the mouth like rabid dogs. The description made me want to puke, cry, and scream simultaneously.

I would have likened it to a Hieronymus Bosch painting instead of a horror movie.

According to their reports, Calvin didn't waste any time. He looked at the guys and said, "Well, boys, it looks like we are going to have to deliver the fucking pain first." And deliver they did.

From the sounds of it, Calvin was like a one-man army, guns blazing and sword swinging. He took down two demons before anyone could blink. And let's not forget some of the color commentary he added. "Oh, so you're the motherfucker that likes to eat human guts. I got something for you!" I mean, who says that? Yeah, that would be Calvin.

Hmph. A John Wick wannabe.

Jeremy was right there with him, crossbow in hand and apparently shooting like some medieval badass. He took a hit to the chest that would've put most people down for the count, but said it only pissed him off more.

The way Calvin told it, Jeremy moved like he wasn't human anymore. He threw knives, punched demons, and sliced throats like it was just another Tuesday for him. And the things he said? "Never let a wild dog sense fear." Who are these guys?

William Tell with a crossbow. One shot, one kill. Then he got scratched and suddenly hulked out like Bruce Banner on steroids.

Rob was on loan from another team and acting as their medic. He took down a demon with a sword through its back but got hurt. Bad. The look on Jeremy's face as he recounted holding Rob and trying to comfort him in his last moments broke my heart. Rob's last words? "I got them. I'm always the medic, and they were my first kills." Fuck, I cried.

The worst part? No survivors. Not one of the innocent people they tried to save made it. I wanted to scream and rage against the unfairness of it all. What good would that do? This is our reality now, and it's fucking brutal.

Korbin, Derek, and Sebastian had the worst part of this mission. Some roving guards at a warehouse near LAX found the bus with one child deceased. One guard called it in but went radio silent afterward.

The team made it there and discovered close to fifteen kids still alive on the bus and a couple more injured. Then the demons in the warehouse made their presence known, and there were plenty to go around.

Derek added that before they got on scene, he asked Korbin, "What if the demon hasn't fully taken the human yet? But they are the ones that did it?" Korbin took a deep breath, looked at Derek, and responded, "Double-tap the son of a bitch right between the eyes."

They went up against at least a dozen demons. Guns, swords, knives…they used everything in a desperate fight for survival but lost Sebastian to being gutted by a demon. That was after Sebastian saved Derek's life.

He shared what Korbin said to one demon before he killed it by kicking it and impaling it on rebar. "You think you can come into our city and attack our children? Destroy our world and get away with it? You are out of your *goddamned* mind."

Derek, the crazy son of a bitch, used a demon as a stripper pole before killing it. Who the hell *does* that? He added that Korbin grumbled at him for "playing a game or two with the demon over there" and asked, "You mind maybe just *killing* the fucking thing so we can be done with it?" beforehand.

That might have been comical to see.

But the aftermath…God, the aftermath.

I didn't know Sebastian, but he saved Derek's life, and now he's gone. Just like that. Another life snuffed out in this endless war against the demons. Korbin stayed at the scene to deal with the police but had Derek bring Sebastian back to the base and alert his team for a proper burial.

What's the point of it all? Why do we keep fighting when it

seems like we're only delaying the inevitable? Then I think about those kids Korbin and his team saved. Fifteen souls might have been lost forever if not for them.

Fifteen souls saved is a Pyrrhic victory, but you'll feel how you feel.

Maybe that's the point. Perhaps it's not about winning the war but about saving who we can when we can. It's a small comfort, but it's something to hold onto in the darkness.

I was sitting at the table, staring out the window when Korbin arrived later that night.

He walked in, and I stood and wrapped my arms around him. "I'm sorry," I whispered. "I know you feel the rage." God, did I know. The anger, the frustration, the feeling of helplessness—it was all too familiar.

"I do," he said, pulling back from me.

I looked up at him, trying to offer some comfort. "It's okay to feel that way. I understand."

Then he dropped a bombshell on me. Five million dollars. A fucking gift to the company. I was speechless. All I could do was exclaim, "Korbin! I don't know what to say."

His response was chilling. "Just make sure that Joshua has every damned thing he needs." He turned away as the anger of the day built again. As he walked away, he glanced back, his eyes bright red. "*Anything* that is needed," he added before disappearing down the hall.

I stood there, stunned. The weight of responsibility settled on my shoulders like a lead blanket. Five million dollars...that's a lot of pressure. If it means we can prevent another massacre like today, I'll take it.

Korbin is a walking powder keg of rage and guilt. He lost two men in this clusterfuck of an operation, and it's eating away at him like acid. He tried to assuage his conscience by throwing money at the problem, but it won't bring back the dead or erase the sight of those lifeless children.

I almost feel sorry for him, but my sympathy evaporates faster than a snowflake in Hell every time I remember he's a pawn in this cosmic chess game.

I don't know what tomorrow will bring. More demons? More death? Probably. I also know that as long as there are people like us out there fighting, we have a chance. A small one, maybe, but a chance nonetheless.

Here's to another day in this demon-infested hellscape. May we live to see another sunrise and never lose sight of our humanity in the face of such overwhelming darkness.

If I ever see Pandora again, I swear to God I'll punch her in her smug face. This is all her fault, and I hope she's rotting in whatever demon-infested hole she crawled into. Bitch.

CHAPTER TWENTY-FOUR

The next week was rough. We were all still reeling from what people were calling "the Los Angeles Massacre." Damian was trying his best to hold us all together, but I saw the grief in his eyes.

Tonight was the ceremony—a rite of passage and a goodbye for those we lost. The atmosphere in the restaurant was weird. We were celebrating the demons we'd killed but mourning those we lost. It felt wrong, somehow.

I'd been chosen to give the speech again. Lucky me. As I stood there in the black dress Pandora had insisted on, I thought about how fucked up this all was. Two more fallen brothers in such a short time. It felt like things were spiraling out of control, like the demons were getting stronger and we were struggling to keep up.

When Damian whispered that it was time, I nodded, approached the mic, and took a deep breath.

"Thank you, everyone, for coming here tonight, both in celebration and remembrance. The LA Massacre left many things unanswered, and we lost several beautiful lives in the process, including three tiny souls. Among the dead were two of our finest, Rob Taylor and Sebastian Alexander..."

I continued with the speech, my voice steady despite my heartache. When I got to the part about reading the poem again, I was surprised to hear a couple of voices join in. It was comforting, in a way. A reminder that we're all in this together.

After the ceremony, I couldn't sleep. I ended up in the kitchen, staring out at the city lights. They were beautiful, constant. No matter what we lost or what happened, those lights kept shining in the distance. It was oddly reassuring.

Then Pandora told me she had something to say, and I'd need something stronger than tea to drink. I grabbed the bottle of bourbon and a rocks glass and took the elevator to the roof for some privacy.

My demon dropped a bombshell on me. She told me about her past, about being part of a group planning to attack Earth. Her brother T'Chezz—what kind of name is that anyway?—had betrayed her and sent her into the circle that brought her here.

"Don't take it personally," she said. "I'm a demon; I did demon things. What other choice did I have? Knitting?"

I snarked, "I'm sure it is warm enough where you come from to do pottery or even cooking. I don't think the only choice was to plan a mass slaughter on all humans on Earth including the elderly and children. I mean, that's how I figured choices worked. But your brother...he sounds like a real douchebag."

Pandora explained that her brother had hoped I'd be an easy target so he could kill her in human form and send her deeper into Hell. "Unfortunately for him, you didn't turn out to be a useless meat bag and easily killed. You are strong and intelligent, and you have a modicum of natural power in you."

I wasn't sure how to take that compliment if you could call it that. Then Pandora dropped another bomb. Her brother would eventually come to ensure she was dead. Which meant he'd be coming for me.

T'Chezz is a fool and underestimates me as usual. He forgets that I'm one of the Seventy-Two, that my power isn't easily extinguished. He certainly doesn't know about you and I forming an unlikely alliance and what we are capable of together.

I flinched at the thought and downed my drink in one go. As I stared at the empty glass, watching the city lights refract through it, I had a moment of clarity. If I could make the lights move the way I wanted, couldn't I do the same with my fate?

I grabbed the bourbon bottle and took a swig straight from it. "Well, fuck." I sniffled. "Fuck him, then."

Music to my ears, truly. It seems we're on the same page about facing this threat head-on.

After a moment of silence, I added, "I guess it's time I try a bit harder, too."

Sitting there on the rooftop, staring at the moon and the desert, I made a decision. I wasn't going to let Pandora's asshole brother get to either of us. We were in this together now, for better or worse.

Something shifted as we sat there in silence. A resolve, perhaps. A determination to not just survive but to thrive in the face of this new challenge. You're right—it's time we both try harder.

Of course, I couldn't let the moment stay serious for too long. I had to point out her unintentional innuendo.

As I took another swig from the bottle, Pandora piped up again. "Psst." She snickered. "You said 'harder.'"

I smiled and shook my head. "Pandora, you are incorrigible."

What can I say? I'm a demon of simple pleasures.

You know what? Maybe that's exactly what I need right now. A bit of inappropriate humor in the face of all this darkness. Because if we can't laugh, even a little, what's the point of fighting at all?

So here's to trying harder, to facing whatever comes our way, and to maybe finding a way to make our own destiny in this fucked-up world of demons and darkness.

For the first time in eons, I feel truly alive. Bring it on, T'Chezz. I'm waiting, and I have one hell of a surprise for you.

AUTHOR NOTES: MICHAEL TODD

Thank you for not only reading the book but also taking the time to look at these author notes. Your interest is appreciated.

On Writing Demons

I'd like to share some thoughts on creativity and writing about demons, a topic that's particularly relevant to this series. My journey to this point has been an interesting one, shaped by a diverse religious background and a variety of life experiences.

In my early years, I was raised in the Catholic faith. Around the age of 8-10, there was a shift to Southern Baptist, and later, at about 14, I found myself in a Baptist church that emphasized 'holy spirit' type beliefs. This religious journey, with its varying perspectives on spirituality and the supernatural, has undoubtedly influenced my writing.

As I've grown and evolved as a writer, I've found myself drawing from a unique combination of influences. My Southern Baptist background, military stories I've read (not in the military myself), interest in D&D and mythology, and yes, my somewhat cynical and occasionally edgy adult humor, have all played a role in shaping this series.

It's an eclectic mix, to be sure. The result is a narrative that blends elements of traditional religious concepts with fantasy mythology and a dash of irreverent humor. It's a balance that I've found both challenging and rewarding to strike.

I realize this series might be a departure from what some of my regular readers expect. It's why I chose to use my first and middle name for this series. The content here is a bit more... let's say 'colorful'... than what you might find in my other works. I wanted to give fair warning to those who might be surprised by the shift in tone.

Writing about demons, especially with my religious background, has been an interesting exercise in creativity. It's allowed me to explore themes and ideas from a different angle, to push boundaries and challenge preconceptions – including my own.

For those of you who've followed me to this new territory, thank you. I hope you find the journey as intriguing as I have. And for new readers joining me for the first time with this series, welcome. I hope you enjoy this blend of the sacred, the profane, and the occasionally ridiculous.

As always, I appreciate your support and your willingness to accompany me on these literary adventures.

Ad Aeternitatem,
Michael

P.S. If you're a glutton for punishment and want more of... whatever this is, don't forget to subscribe to my newsletter. It's like these author notes, but with more typos. Check it out here: https://michael.beehiiv.com/

BOOKS BY MICHAEL ANDERLE

Sign up for the LMBPN email list to be notified of new releases and special deals!

https://lmbpn.com/email/

For a complete list of books by Michael Anderle, please visit:

www.lmbpn.com/ma-books/

CONNECT WITH THE AUTHOR

Connect with Michael Anderle

Website: http://lmbpn.com

Email List: https://michael.beehiiv.com/

https://www.facebook.com/LMBPNPublishing

https://twitter.com/MichaelAnderle

https://www.instagram.com/lmbpn_publishing/

https://www.bookbub.com/authors/michael-anderle

9 7 9 8 8 8 9 1 4 6 1 6 7 3